COOPER & PACKRAT

Mystery of the Bear Cub

The Cooper & Packrat Adventures

Book 1: *Mystery on Pine Lake*
A Junior Library Guild Selection
2014 Maine State Book Award Finalist
2016-2017 Massachusetts Children's Book Award Finalist

Someone is out to harm a family of loons. Cooper Wilder and his new best friend, Packrat, must find the culprit and protect the nest.

Book 2: *Mystery of the Eagle's Nest*
A Junior Library Guild Selection
2015 Green Earth Book Award Short List

Cooper and Packrat get caught in the middle of illegal trading of eagle parts and the kidnapping of a baby eaglet.

Book 3: *Mystery of the Missing Fox*
A Junior Library Guild Selection

Cooper, Packrat, and Roy must protect a fox den, save the kits, and rule out Summer, the new girl who lives across the lake, as a suspect.

COOPER & PACKRAT

Mystery
of the
Bear Cub

By Tamra Wight
Illustrations by Carl DiRocco

ISLANDPORT PRESS

ISLANDPORT PRESS

P. O. Box 10
Yarmouth, Maine 04096
www.islandportpress.com
books@islandportpress.com

ISBN: 978-1-944762-25-4
Library of Congress Control Number: 2017935693
Printed in the USA

Dean L. Lunt, Publisher
Front cover, back cover, and interior art: Carl DiRocco
Book design: Teresa Lagrange / Islandport Press

To the staff and campers of Poland Spring Campground,
especially my young campers.

Never lose your sense of wonder and adventure.

Chapter 1

Black bears may be active at any time of the day or night.

I took the skinny, wiggly worm from my bait bucket and slid it onto my fishing hook. No matter how many times I did it, I still cringed a little. Lifting the fishing rod up over my head, I lowered it back over my shoulder, then whipped it forward while releasing the line. The red-and-white bobber soared through the air before landing with a plop among the lily pads in the cove.

"Nice cast!" Packrat said from behind me in our canoe.

I looked back at my friend. Under his life jacket, he was wearing a vest of many pockets over his T-shirt. I still hadn't gotten used to seeing him in it. From the very first day I'd met him, when he and his mom had towed their travel trailer into my family's campground to spend the summer, he'd always worn a trench coat of many pockets. You name it, he had it in that coat!

This past winter, though, an old flight vest at his church's thrift store had caught his eye. "Way better on hot days," he'd told me. "And almost as many pockets, too!"

Since the campground bathrooms were clean and the sites were raked, my dad had given us the rest of the day off. We didn't have much business at Wilder Family Campground in June, so the jobs didn't take as long. Of course, our paychecks weren't so big either. But we didn't care. Once Fourth of July arrived, and all the campers started rolling through our gate, two things would happen: One, we'd be clocking in some serious work hours; and two, Packrat, Roy, and I would be begging and scheming for big chunks of time out on the lake. So right now, this minute, Packrat and I felt pretty lucky. I raised my face to the sun, closed my eyes, and soaked up the warm almost-summer rays.

"When are Roy and his mom and dad moving into their camper?" Packrat's voice brought me back to earth.

I turned in my seat so I could see him as he fished. "Today's his last day of school." I chuckled. "He was pretty mad when he heard we got out two days before him."

Packrat laughed with me and reeled in his line a little bit.

I tugged on mine, making the bobber dance on the surface of the water. "His dad's driving him up tomorrow."

Packrat raised an eyebrow. "His dad? You think he'll actually spend the night this time?"

I shrugged. Mr. Parker hardly ever came up from Portland with Roy and his mom. According to Roy, his dad didn't like camping. He liked the city, and his job there, better.

The sun climbed a little higher. Not a leaf twitched. Not a pine-cone stirred. This cove was protected from the wind, which made it an excellent fishing spot. It was always way warmer, in this semicircle of trees, than out in the middle of the lake. And today, with the tempera-ture hovering around 75 degrees, it felt downright hot. My eyelids got heavy. I struggled to open them, to see my bobber. They slid closed.

Hissssssssss!

Probably some kind of bug, I thought, keeping my eyes closed.

HISS! Splash. Hisssssssss!

I sat up so fast the canoe rocked back and forth, making me bobble my fishing pole. It clattered to the floor as I grabbed hold of the canoe's sides with both hands. "What was that?"

Packrat's squinting eyes scanned the surface of the water, trying to see into the shadows of the cove.

Splash. Splash. SPLASH!

A huge claw-like thing, about the size of my palm, rose up out of the water. It was a dark brownish-green with nails about an inch and a half long.

Sharp nails!

It hung there, reaching for the sky. Packrat and I leaned forward.

A long, skinny blob the size and shape of my fist rose up next. It had nostrils, two eyes, two teeth, and a mouth. An oval shell. A turtle! But not just any turtle.

A snapping turtle!

Packrat and I slowly paddled forward as the claw connected with the turtle head.

Hisssssssss!

The head, the shell, and the claw all sank under the water like a submarine. Was it in trouble? Why would it hit itself in the head like that?

We paddled a little closer. And a little closer still. *Two* turtle heads rose up out of the water! One opened its mouth wide, its head stretching farther and farther from its shell, all slow-motion-like. Then it lunged for the other turtle's face.

A turtle fight!

"Whoa!" breathed Packrat. He put his pole down to dig into one of his vest pockets. "Have you ever seen anything like this before?"

"Never!" I replied.

Pulling out a camera, he began recording.

Both heads sunk under the water again, then rose again, higher this time. A claw came up and connected with the other head, covering its eye and dragging downward, leaving a gash.

"Ow!" Packrat winced. "That's gotta hurt. Should we break it up?"

"It's nature." But if it got any worse, I was thinking I might put a paddle between them.

The underdog, or under-turtle, rose up once more. It laid a claw on the other turtle's neck. That turtle quickly rolled and went under.

"Are you getting all this?" I cried. Roy was going to love it!

Packrat nodded. His eye on the camera screen, he zoomed in.

Up went another claw. The nails extended as far as they could go. "That," I shuddered, "is going to give me nightmares tonight when we sleep in the tent."

Packrat chuckled. Then he frowned. His brows furrowed as he tilted the camera to point it over both turtles' heads.

"There's something," he muttered, "in the water. By the shore."

I turned in the direction the camera was pointing, toward a dark, shady stretch of shoreline with low-hanging maple tree branches over it. "I don't—"

There! A big black mound moved soundlessly through the water. It was too big to be a beaver or an otter. It was too small to be a moose. At this distance, I couldn't get a good look at all its details. I couldn't tell if it had ears or fur. Turtle fight forgotten, I shaded my eyes and squinted. Whatever this was, it slowly padded out of the water on all fours, then shook off, before plodding into the woods.

"Fur," I said. "It definitely had fur."

Packrat took the camera and turned it around to see the view screen. He touched a button and the video replayed. He replayed it one more time.

"A dog?" he wondered out loud. Moving to sit on the middle bench, closer to me, he added, "Nah, It's too big."

"Well, those Portuguese water dogs are huge! Bigger than a Great Dane. More like a small pony. But what's it doing swimming here? I mean, no one lives on that side of the lake."

"Maybe it's lost?" Packrat suggested.

We watched the video again. Then once more.

Packrat and I looked at each other over the camera.

"Only one way we're gonna find out." I picked up my fishing pole and reeled in my line, realizing that the turtles had left.

Packrat nodded. He moved to his seat at the back of the canoe and did the same.

Then the two of us dipped our paddles in the water and headed for the spot where the maybe-dog had crawled out.

Chapter 2

Sometimes, bears use trails created by generations of bears before them, literally stepping in the well-worn footprints of their mothers and grandmothers who came before them.

Packrat and I found a little sandy area to bank the canoe. I jumped out of the front of the canoe, onto land, then pulled it up a little farther. Trying to keep his feet dry, Packrat walked the length of the canoe and stepped out onto the mini beach.

I unclipped my life jacket and looked around. There was nothing but woods as far as I could see. Two rocks, the size of picnic tables, sat side by side at the tree line. Cutting right between them was a little trail leading into the woods.

"Ever been here before?" Packrat asked.

"Nope," I said, throwing my life jacket into the canoe. "Wanna see where the trail goes?"

"Does a bear poop in the woods?"

"Yes!" We said it at the same time. My friend laughed at his own joke as he threw his life jacket in with mine.

I took one side of the canoe, Packrat took the other, and we pulled it even farther up on land, until it was half-hidden under some bushes.

"This trail isn't marked like the red-blazed one we made in your campground," Packrat said, as we stepped past the rocks and into the woods. "Is this still your property?"

"I think so, but it's a piece that doesn't have campsites yet." I looked around at all the maples, birches, pines, and oak trees in all sizes and ages, from seedling to hundreds of years old. "I don't know this trail. I'm thinking it's a wildlife one, made by deer, moose, and fox—you know, when they go back and forth to get a drink at the lake or take a bath."

We walked single file, stopping every now and then to look at interesting stuff like frogs, animal scat, or bugs. Eventually, we came to an uprooted tree, its three-foot-wide trunk lying across the trail. I threw one leg over it, and there, through the woods, a sparkle caught my eye. I threw my other leg over and put both feet on the ground. "Hey, I'm checking something out!" I called as I headed off-trail toward it.

The sparkling drew me to a fallen-down section of rock wall—not the fancy kind of rock wall where all the rocks lie perfectly flat, one on top of the other. This was an old wall with rocks of every size, shape, and color. The cracks were full of leaves, pine needles, and dirt. The rocks were spotted with gray and green moss.

I stepped through the broken section and searched the ground. There, half in and half out of the forest floor, I could see part of a clear but dirty bottle. It lay at the top of a small banking that sloped downward. The sunlight must have hit it just right to make it twinkle, because it was anything but shiny. Inside of it there were brown leaves and a layer of black dirt.

I turned to leave. But then I had two thoughts: One, just because someone else dropped their trash and left it here didn't mean that I had to leave it here; and two, what if an animal stepped on it by accident? Or that dog?

I turned back. Putting two fingers inside the top, I cautiously tried to lift it out of the leaves. But it wouldn't give, so I got down on my knees. Carefully, I pushed all the leaves aside, to find the bottle was half buried in the dirt. I dug under one side of it with my fingertips to loosen it. And dug some more. And even more. When it finally wiggled a bit, I tugged up and lifted it out. It was whole! I turned it over in my hands. It looked like an old milk bottle, the kind Grandma had told me about from the days when milk was delivered to your house. Inside, there were three white spider-egg sacs stuck to the side. The raised markings on the glass itself were a little worn down and hard to read.

Cooper and Packrat: Mystery of the Bear Cub

Looking back at the hole the bottle had left, I could see more glass. I couldn't help it; I had to know what else was there! Very carefully, I dug around the sides, scooping out dark brown, moist, forest-floor dirt. This time, I pulled a smaller, clear-glass bottle, half the size of the other, from the dirt. This one had a one-inch neck with a dotted ridge on the end. Seeing more clear glass to the right, I dug at that, but it turned out to be a boring old jar, kind of the shape of a canning jar. Just as I put my hand on the ground to stand, I saw something blue in the hole I'd made. I started digging again. Ten minutes later, I was pulling out a light blue bottle, pear-shaped, about seven inches high. As I brushed off the dirt, I could see raised lines in the glass: two twirls, side by side.

"Hey, Coop," Packrat called through the trees, "you gotta see this!"

I looked up, but I couldn't see him. Where the heck had he gone? Picking up my bottles, I half-walked, half-jogged in the direction he'd taken. Two minutes later, I found myself in the middle of an old rectangular cellar hole, just about the size of our basement. Two and a half walls still stood: a short end and a long end, which were mostly built into the side of a small hill. While they were kind of crumbly, they were intact. The other long side that had been freestanding had half-fallen down. And the fourth side, a short end, had totally fallen.

The walls that still stood were taller than me, and made from flat rocks. The house or barn that once sat on top of it was long gone, of course. A few weedy plants poked up from the cellar floor, which had probably been dirt. I scuffed my toe and found there was a thick layer of leaves with dark rich dirt underneath.

In the middle of the short, fallen end was one of the biggest fieldstone fireplaces I'd ever seen. Some of the corners were broken or missing, and the whole thing looked worn and weathered, but the rest of it stood tall. The place where you build the fire, the firebox, was open on both sides and was large enough to fit a regular kitchen stove. Seeing a pair of sneaker tips sticking out from where I thought the firebox wall would be, I bent at the waist, stepped inside, and found that I could stand up! Turning, I found these inside walls went back just far enough for Packrat to stand with his back against it, and be hidden. Well, except for his toes. I grinned at him. "Found you!"

"Wouldn't this be an awesome hiding spot for Capture the Flag?" he exclaimed. "Roy would never find us."

We stepped back outside. "Do you know who lived here?" Packrat asked, turning in a circle, checking everything out.

I shook my head. We stepped through what would have been a cellar-door space in the wall. "First time I've seen it." We walked around the outside, looking for clues of who had lived here or what this place had been—

"Watch out!" Packrat grabbed my shirt, hauling me backward. "You almost fell in!"

I'd been so busy looking at the cellar walls that I hadn't seen the four-foot-wide hole in the ground, surrounded by rocks. Filled to the top with water, it looked pretty deep. I knelt, put my hand in the water, and felt around. The sides were lined with rocks, too.

I frowned. "A well?"

Packrat crouched down next to me to study it. "That's my guess." He took out a small measuring tape from an inside pocket. Pulling out the end, he stuck it into the center of the well. He kept pulling and pulling, the tape going down and down into the water. "Three feet. Four feet. Seven feet." When there was no more tape to pull, he whistled. "Ten feet! Maybe more! It still isn't touching bottom!"

I put my hand on his shoulder. "You'd better back up; the sides might cave in. I bet this is one of those old hand-dug wells." I stood, and turned slowly in a circle. "I wonder how long all this has been here?"

"And why was it abandoned?" my friend wondered.

We searched the area, but besides the spot where I'd found the bottles, the cellar hole, fireplace, and the well, the only other thing we found was a little bit of deer scat. I gathered up my glass bottles while Packrat put away his measuring tape, and we headed back to the trail. Packrat started to go left, deeper into the woods. But I looked at my watch. "Uh-oh. We're gonna be late."

Packrat groaned. "Already?" But he turned with me to hike back toward our canoe. The campground walkie-talkie radio wasn't strong enough to keep contact with the campground office, but my worrywart mom wouldn't take that for an excuse anymore if I was late. I pulled out my phone. "Huh. No signal here."

Packrat pulled his own phone out of a top outside pocket. "Me neither."

Saying Mom was not going to be happy with us was like saying bee stings only hurt a tiny bit.

As we stepped out from the woods into the sun-soaked shoreline, bright orange tiger lilies caught my eye. Seeing them growing wild on the shoreline like that, I wondered if they'd been there since the cellar-owning family had lived here. I imagined their seeds rolling, tumbling, and flying season after season through the years to get to this spot.

I dropped my sweatshirt in the middle of the canoe, and laid the four bottles on it for safekeeping.

"The blue one's really cool," Packrat said, picking up his life jacket and putting his arms through it. "It'll look awesome once you clean it up."

I looked at it again, suddenly hit with a genius idea. "Be right back," I told my friend.

Jogging to the wild tiger lilies, I pulled out my pocketknife and cut three of them. On my way back, I saw Packrat raise an eyebrow and smirk. "You got a girlfriend I don't know about?"

I snorted so hard I dropped my knife. Bending over, I grabbed it, and froze. Right there in the sand, in front of my sneaker, was an animal footprint. And not just any old footprint.

I heard Packrat suck in a little breath. I shaded my eyes and scanned the woods.

"Maybe we'd better go," Packrat said. He grabbed one side of the canoe and started pushing it toward the water. He stopped. Sighed. And pulled out his camera.

Putting his own foot up against the animal print to show its length, he snapped a picture. Next, he crouched down to take a close-up. All the while, he kept one eye on the path to the woods.

"Don't worry," I said. But I wasn't sure who I was trying to calm down, Packrat or myself. The print was about six inches long. The main part was cashew-shaped. Above that were five toe marks, each one with a claw mark above it. "They don't want to bump into us any more than we want to bump into them."

Watching loons, eagles, foxes, turtles, beavers, and frogs was really cool.

Watching an adult black bear would be wicked cool, too.

But only if we were watching from a distance.

Chapter 3

A mother bear is very attentive to her cubs during their first spring and summer. Not only does she check on them constantly, but she also gets upset if they're missing, and comes running if they whine. Although rare, a mother bear will even carry her cubs on her back.

"You boys are the sweetest!" Mom couldn't stop arranging and rearranging the tiger lilies in the light blue bottle. I'd scrubbed all the years and years and years of dirt from it until it shone. "I can't believe you stopped to pick them for me." Mom was proudly displaying them on the campground office registration counter.

"And that's why we're late," I explained. "I'm sorry we weren't back on time to——"

"Don't you worry about that." Mom leaned in to sniff the flowers for the gazillionth time. I'm surprised she hadn't sniffed the colors right off them yet.

Packrat gave me a sideways I-can't-believe-that-worked look as Mom slid the flowers down the counter to sit right next to the cash register, where everyone would see them. Packrat's mom, who was back to help my mom for another summer, sighed heavily as she dusted a small wooden loon carving. She put it down and picked up another. Eyes twinkling, Stacey teased, "If only I had a son who thought to bring me flowers."

Packrat gave me a pretend-annoyed look. "Now look what you started," he joked.

Hearing the store's screen door open, I turned to look.

Now, when one of your middle school teachers shows up at your campground unexpectedly, just three days into summer vacation, that could only mean two things: One, you didn't pass seventh grade like you thought; or two, she was there to camp. Which would be kind of weird.

But I'd rather have weird than repeat seventh grade.

Ms. Marco caught my eye and headed straight for me. With her was a man who looked kind of familiar. He had on a white button-down shirt, jeans, and dress shoes.

Please let her be here to camp, please let her be here to camp, I chanted in my head. Seeing a typed paper in my English teacher's hand, I sucked in a breath.

That was mine!

Worry must have been written all over my face like the words on that report, because Ms. Marco laughed. "You aren't in trouble, Cooper Wilder. Quite the opposite."

The man held out his hand to me. I was wicked confused, but I took it. "Tim Talbot!" the man grasped my hand firmly and shook it. "Town manager. Nice to finally meet you!"

Ms. Marco laid my paper on the registration counter. The title jumped out at me. *The Importance of Whole Town Recycling.* Persuasive essays had been the last assignment Ms. Marco had given my class. We were supposed to pick a topic important to us, choose whether we were for or against it, and write the paper as if we were trying to get someone to agree with us. I couldn't help smiling when I saw the big, fat, red A+ across page one. I looked from it, to the man, to Ms. Marco.

Mom picked up her coffee mug, her eyes twinkling. "So what's my son done this time?" she asked, before taking a sip.

Packrat came into the office and stood beside me. Ms. Marco laughed at Mom's joke. "Tim, would you like to do the honors?"

Would somebody just tell me what the heck was going on? Luckily, I only screamed that in my head.

Mr. Talbot cleared his throat in that I'm-about-to-say-something-important way. He put his hands in his pockets and rocked back on his heels. "Cooper, I was really, really impressed with your report." He pulled a hand from his pocket to tap my report several times with his pointer finger. "Very clever. Lots of facts. Very . . ."—he paused, his eyes staring up at the ceiling as he searched for the right word—". . . doable."

Mom's brows came together. She set her mug on the counter and reached for my essay. Packrat moved around the counter to read with her. Even Packrat's mom had stopped dusting to listen. Mr. Talbot kept talking. "I've been looking for a new project, something to help our town. Something the landowners could rally behind." He pointed at the paper Mom was reading. "This is it!"

"Recycling?" I was still confused.

"Not just the recycling. Although I had no idea fishing line didn't decompose for six hundred years!" He shook his head. "It was your *plan* for recycling that impressed me. I'd really like to bring your idea before the townspeople and see if we can get it voted in. Truth be told, I already kind of, sort of, talked to some. To feel them out, you know? They loved the idea. Loved it! But I thought I'd check with you personally," he said, "to be sure you were okay with my using your idea. I'll give you full credit, of course." He grabbed my shoulder and gave it a gentle squeeze.

Packrat took the paper from Mom's hands. "Whoa. Soda cans don't go away for a hundred years?"

Ms. Marco nodded. "Those are the facts that made me sit up and take notice, too! When I read about all those things, the ones that take hundreds of years to decompose? Well, I knew we had to do something."

"But I—" The screen door slammed shut, and Mom looked up and over my head. The rest of us turned to see a woman walk in. She had long black hair, tied back in a single ponytail. Behind her trailed a kid a little younger than us. His eyes went right to Packrat's mom and the tall wooden eagle she was now dusting. I knew that I-just-want-to-hold-it look. The woman put a hand on the back of his black-haired head when he started to walk over. He turned back to her and she raised an eyebrow. I knew that look, too. It was the don't-even-think-about-it look.

Mom shot a worried glance from Mr. Talbot, to me, over to the new people.

"Do you want me to—" Packrat's mom started to ask.

Mom's customer-service side kicked in. "No, you go ahead and finish up. I've got it." To me she whispered "I'll be right back," before moving down the counter to wait on them.

"We pick up trash from the cans on the campsites," Packrat began. "Then your dad takes it all to the town dump—I mean, transfer station. It has recycling, right?"

"It does," Mr. Talbot explained. "But it's not mandatory. It's a choice. And it's only the basics."

"We were there once," Packrat said thoughtfully, "when the trash at the station was getting hauled away to . . ." He frowned. "Where does it go from there?"

"A landfill," I explained. "It gets buried underground."

"Wait. Isn't that bad for the drinking water?"

I shook my head. "Not the one our trash goes to. That one is done in a way that doesn't let the trash leak into our drinking water. But it takes a lot longer for everything to break down." I looked at Ms. Marco. "When I was researching my report, I found out that the landfill our trash goes to will be full by the end of the year. And there isn't another place within fifty miles to build a new one."

Ms. Marco beamed. "So he came up with an idea. Tell them!"

I could feel my ears turning red. "My paper says that our transfer station should do more recycling and sorting. And everyone should *have* to do it. Some of the recyclables could be sold, and that stuff would be made into new stuff. What's left that's not recyclable would go to an incinerator. There's a new one I found; it burns trash to create electricity and heat. And burning keeps the trash from ending up in the ground. But—"

"Your plan is brilliant!" Mr. Talbot cut me off. He looked at his watch. "I'd like to present this tomorrow at the town meeting. Might as well get it all approved right away. It'll take time to upgrade our little old transfer station to do more recycling. Will you come? I'd like to give credit where credit is due."

I shrugged. "Sure." Although I didn't see how my being there would help get it passed or anything.

Mr. Talbot clapped me on the back. "Great! Great! See you tomorrow at the town hall. Nine o'clock!"

As he and Ms. Marco left the office, I heard her say, "Nine o'clock? Tomorrow morning? Aren't meetings usually at two in the afternoon?"

Mr. Talbot stepped out the door, then turned to hold it open. Dad stepped through. "Tim! Don't tell me we have finally convinced you to try camping?"

The town manager laughed. "Here on business." He winked at me, which had Dad looking back and forth between us. If it were a cartoon scene, there would have been a hundred question marks in every size rising over his head. "Ask your son about it," Mr. Talbot said, and gave me a good-bye nod. "I've got a meeting to get ready for." The door slammed shut behind him.

"We have a site with no electric hookup, no water hookup," Mom was saying to the people at the counter. Smiling gently, she added, "Are you sure? Tenting that way for the whole summer might get pretty old after a while." She held up her pointer finger to show Dad she needed him to wait a minute.

The lady didn't smile back. "It's what we can afford," she said simply. Taking the pen off the counter, she began writing her information on the registration form.

The kid took a small step away. Then another. Without looking up, the woman reached out with her free hand to pull him back. In a whisper she said, "Charlie Connor, you stay here."

"But——" said the kid.

"We don't have any extra money, and that's that," she said, never looking up from the form.

Mom moved down to stand by Dad and me, to give them some privacy. Dad took off his baseball cap and ran his hand through his hair. "What'd Tim want?"

The way Dad asked, he looked all casual and stuff. But there was something else in his voice, too. I started to explain. Mom handed Dad my paper. I finished my story, but he kept reading. From the corner of my eye, I noticed Charlie silently slip away, heading for the souvenir section. When he got to it, he looked over at his mom, who was counting her money out on the counter. The kid reached out a hand toward the wooden loon. Pausing, he looked over his shoulder, and seeing me watching him, he ducked his head and put his hand back in his pocket.

"So your plan here is that our town's transfer station needs to have more recycling?" Dad's voice had me looking back at him. "And everyone has to do it."

I nodded.

"It's a good idea, son." Dad hesitated.

"It really is," Mom agreed.

Packrat punched me in the arm. "You're going to be a town hero!"

My friend obviously hadn't heard the "but" in my parents' voices.

Dad shook his head. "With some people, you'll be a hero. But Cooper . . ."

Here it came.

"At our campground, we can't force one hundred and thirty-two families to recycle their trash every day. And I don't want to be the one to sort through the hundreds of bags of trash we collect from the campsite trash cans. Twice a week." Dad paused and raised an eyebrow. "Do you?"

Chapter 4

Black bears eat almost anything, including plants, fruit, insects, seeds, nuts, birds, and small mammals.

I stood in the back of the dump truck with slimy, oozing trash bags up to my armpits. No matter how hard I tried to move through the bags, my left foot stayed stuck to the bed of the truck. The other kept slipping and sliding in something really gooey. I didn't even want to know what had seeped through my sneakers and socks, and was making my ankles sting.

On my left, two little, black, beady lobster eyes looked out at me from a rip in a clear trash bag. To my right, leftover spaghetti and tomato sauce slowly dripped down the outside of another bag.

"Throw down another, Cooper!" Dad called.

I lifted the bag closest to me and tossed it over the side. Packrat caught it, then dropped it at Dad's feet. Dad untied it and started pulling stuff out, one thing at a time. "Green bean can goes in recycling. This apple core goes in the trash to be burned. Recycling. Trash. Trash."

"Fifty bags done," Packrat called up to me. "Only five hundred and sixty-three more to go." He held out his hands. "Throw another!"

This time, I tossed the bag a little too far. He jumped up, and as his hands grabbed for it, the bag split open and emptied on his head. Sour-smelling curdled milk ran down his face and dripped off his nose. One, two, three meatballs bounced off his white sneakers.

Packrat's sad, trash-covered face looked up at me. It flickered. It wavered. And suddenly, Mr. Talbot was in his place. "Great job, Wilder Family Campground! Don't you feel better knowing you're doing your part to recycle?"

Bags of trash started raining down on me. Black bags, green bags, clear bags, little bags, until I was up to my chin in them.

"Throw down another, Cooper!" Dad hollered. But I couldn't move. My legs and arms were frozen—

"Cooper! Cooper! Wake up!" My little sister Molly's voice came from far away.

A dream? But . . . my legs! They still wouldn't move! I struggled to open my eyes. Hearing a giggle, I realized I was stuck, not because I was buried in trash bags, but because Molly was actually in the tent, sitting on my legs. "It's seven o'clock," she said. "And you wanted me to wake you at seven."

I poked her in her side, sending her into a fit of giggles. She rolled off me and onto the blob in the next sleeping bag that was Packrat. He just groaned and burrowed deeper in his bag.

Molly sat up. "I almost forgot! Mom said to give you these." She reached over me to pick up a slightly crumpled paper bag. Inside, I saw two squished flat, but still warm, banana muffins. I looked at her and raised my eyebrows.

Molly giggled. "I went down the slide a couple times on the way here. With the bag. Sorry."

I laughed, but didn't ask for details. I didn't want to know. "They'll taste the same. Go on, tell Mom we'll be right out to clean the bathrooms."

"Okay."

As she scooted out the tent flap, I nudged the Packrat lump in the sleeping bag next to me. My mind was still on the dream and today's town meeting.

My sweatshirt around my neck, I poked Packrat again. He moaned. He stretched. He groaned and complained his way out of the bag. Sitting up and scratching his head, he said, "Big day, huh?"

I put my arms through my sweatshirt sleeves, nodded, and reached for my sneakers.

"Are you still hoping they'll vote your recycling plan in?" He grabbed his sweatshirt and turned it inside-right.

I concentrated on tugging on my shoes, 'cause I wasn't sure how to answer. "I guess. I mean, I really, really think recycling is important, you know? But . . ."

"But?" Packrat prodded.

"I don't want to make more work for everybody."

"My mom says the easiest way isn't always the right way."

"I know." I crawled over to push back the tent flap. "But when I wrote it, I didn't think anyone would actually *do* it. It was just a project, you know? I really only wrote it because I thought the new incinerator in Bangor was cool, the way it uses the burning to make electricity and heat for their community. And the ash is used by construction companies. If I'd have thought Mr. Talbot would get ahold of my report, I'd have asked Mom and Dad some questions first. Now we've got to make our own plan to get ready for it."

"What? We aren't going to open every trash bag we pick up on the campsites, and sort the stuff inside if your plan passes?" One side of Packrat's mouth was turned up, telling me he was kidding. "Darn, I was looking forward to that."

I thought about the Packrat in my dream and laughed out loud. "There's no way we could do that."

Packrat put on his vest of many pockets and grabbed the paper bag Molly had brought. When we were outside and on our feet, he opened it to pass me my share. "Then the campers have to recycle?"

I took a bite of the warm banana muffin and shook my head. "There's always gonna be some people that won't. My research said about half." I led the way down the camp road, past the office, and headed to the Snack Shack.

Packrat frowned. "That many?"

Big Joe saw us coming and had two steaming cups of cocoa ready to hand us when we got there. "Two chocolate packets in each." He winked at us. Leaning on the counter on his elbows, he said, "Your dad told me about the town meeting today. You and your family have a plan for the campground if it passes?"

I looked into my hot cocoa like it had all the answers, and shook my head.

Big Joe stood tall again, wiping his hands on his apron. "Well, if it does pass, I'm sure you'll figure it out. Good luck today, kid."

I nodded. "Thanks."

I was going to need it.

Chapter 5

Black bears spend most of their waking hours eating or searching for their next meal. They have to gain a lot of weight to prepare for their long winter sleep.

The minute we walked through the tall, white, double doors of the town hall, Mr. Talbot met us with a booming, "Hello there!" He marched Packrat, Dad, and me down the middle aisle to sit in the center row, right in front of the stage. "I want ya close, just in case I have a question!"

Forty minutes later, as the meeting dragged on, no one had even said the word *trash* yet. Dad must have looked around the room six times, muttering, "Where is everyone?" and "Smallest town meeting I've ever been to."

The gentleman behind me must have thought so, too, because he kept grumbling the whole time about how little notice everyone had been given. "It was only posted on the Main Street sign two days ago," he told the guy next to him, and the guy behind him, and the lady across the aisle. "And half the people I told thought it was at the usual two o'clock time."

BANG. BANG. BANG. My eyes looked up to the stage. Five people sat at a long gray table, facing us. Mr. Talbot was smack in the middle, a little wooden hammer-gavel in his hand. "Next on the agenda," he paused for a couple of seconds, beaming at everyone, "is recycling!" I swear he looked like he expected applause or something. What he got was shuffling feet and moving around in seats. Especially by me.

He cleared his throat. "Two weeks ago, Ms. Marco, a teacher from our middle school, sent me a very interesting essay from one of her prize students."

Prize? My ears started getting warm.

Mr. Talbot looked down the table at Ms. Marco and smiled. "It made me take a good hard look at the way we run our town's transfer station." He put his hand around the microphone in front of him and leaned forward in his seat. "We do very little recycling compared to the towns around us. In addition, our town has grown. The amount of trash we're dealing with has grown. Our employees at the transfer station report lines of cars and trucks waiting to get in. And sometimes, they have to close because there's no more room in the hoppers for trash until it's picked up and taken to the landfill. A landfill that itself is almost full." He lifted a pencil and pointed it out into the audience, then at me. "My little friend here, Cooper from Wilder Family Campground—"

Little friend?

"—came up with a plan I'd like to propose to you today."

Everyone looked my way. I squirmed in my seat and looked down at Packrat's swinging feet. In my head I was screaming, *Just explain it already!* I couldn't stand the suspense of wondering what all these people were going to think about the idea. My idea. An idea I never thought would go beyond Ms. Marco's desk.

He explained how they were going to make the transfer station bigger and better. Everyone would be required to use clear plastic bags. Number 2 to Number 6 plastics, tin and metal, paper, cardboard, and more would be recycled in one area. There would be special bins for things like lumber. "As a town, we'll get paid for all the recycling we take to the recycling plant." He beamed at all of us again.

I got brave enough to look over my shoulder. Everyone seemed to be smiling and nodding!

"The trash that can't be recycled will be hauled out of town to the new incinerator in Bangor. Now, we do have to pay them to take it. But what we'll get paid for the recyclables will help with that. And what I like about this plan is that this incinerator turns burning trash into electricity and heat for its communities. Not adding to a landfill can only mean we're doing our part to protect Maine's land and our environment."

I heard the two gentlemen behind me whispering, approving.

"Of course, to do this, we'll have to close down our transfer station for a bit." There was a low murmuring in the room, and not the good kind. Mr. Talbot said quickly, "I know, I know. But we need to restructure the station. We hope it will only be for a week."

"Any questions from the floor?" asked the man sitting at the table to Mr. Talbot's left.

A woman stood up in the back. "I'd like to personally thank Cooper Wilder for this plan. I've been trying to get recycling into this town since I moved here, but no one listened to me!" She started to clap, and the rest of the people in the hall clapped along with her. Everyone was smiling and looking my way. Dad wore a little smile, too. Packrat said, "Yeah! Told ya so! I knew you'd be a hero."

Mr. Talbot banged his gavel. The sound was sharp and hard, but he still wore a smile. A man's hand went up in the audience and he pointed to him. "You have a question, Bert?"

A tall, thin older gentleman stood. He held his hat in his hands, turning it every so often. He cleared his throat three times without saying anything. I kinda felt bad for him, 'cause I guessed public speaking wasn't his thing.

"For the record," Mr. Talbot said, "Mr. Goodwin, owner of one of our oldest town businesses, Goodwin's General Store, has the floor."

Mr. Goodwin cleared his throat again. "And this—er—plan? It would work the same for businesses like mine?"

His business didn't have complicated trash like ours. They only had trash-trash in their little coffee counter and store, not customer-dropped-off trash like us. So I smiled and nodded to Mr. Goodwin, to show him he could still use the town's new transfer station, as long as he recycled.

Mr. Goodwin caught my eye and smiled back.

"Unfortunately, no," Mr. Talbot said into the microphone.

Mr. Goodwin and I looked at each other, and then at Mr. Talbot. I stood up. "But—"

"One of the many things we had to take a long hard look at was how much trash we could afford to haul to this new incinerator station. It's two hours away in Bangor." Murmuring and grumbling came from all over the room. Mr. Talbot banged his gavel. "Between the cost of transporting our trash to the incinerator and then paying them to take it, I'm afraid our little transfer station can only be for residences. Home-owners." He paused to survey the room. "Businesses will have to make other arrangements. I'm sure you'll all understand."

"Understand? Other arrangements?" Mr. Goodwin had found his voice. And it was loud. "But I live in this town. By God, I pay my taxes. On time, too! What do you propose I, and all the other businesspeople like me, do?"

"You could use a dumpster service," Mr. Talbot suggested.

Mr. Goodwin harrumphed. And then he glared at me. In fact, there were lots of eyes glaring at me.

I slunk down in my seat. This was not my plan.

Not my plan at all.

Chapter 6

Bears have been known to take food from pet dishes and bird feeders, even if they are right outside a home.

There was a moment of silence. Then everyone started talking over one another. Business owners argued with homeowners. Even some homeowners thought it was unfair not to allow businesses to use the transfer station.

My dad stood up. Mr. Talbot banged the gavel. "Jim Wilder of Wilder Family Campground has the floor!" He had to say it two more times, and bang the gavel three more, before everyone quieted down to let him speak.

Dad looked directly at Mr. Talbot. "Because of the nature of our business," he said, "and not being in control of what's put into every bag of trash, my business couldn't use the new transfer station anyway. But I strongly disagree with saying all businesses aren't allowed to use it." Dad put his hand out, palm up. "Why couldn't you make the decision business by business? Say, those who can recycle can use it. Those who can't need to make other arrangements."

Mr. Talbot leaned forward in his chair. "We had to make a clear and easy cutoff. We think this is it." He held up his hand in a stop-right-there way when people started to talk again. "Listen! This wasn't an easy decision." He looked up and down the table and everyone there nodded at him, except Ms. Marco. She looked down at her hands, which were clenched on the table. "But I do feel," he said, leaning forward in his chair again, "that our town will save money and be better off environmentally because of it. And what it comes down to, is hauling to the landfill isn't going to be an option anymore. It's closing. We're giving notice. A week from Monday, the transfer station will be closed for upgrades. And when it opens, businesses will no longer be allowed to dump their trash there."

The man to Mr. Talbot's left quickly said, "I'd like to take this to a vote. All in favor of the new recycling package, raise your hand."

Looking around, I saw a lot of hands up. More than I expected. Ms. Marco counted, and when she wrote the number down, Mr. Talbot glanced over at it.

The man running the meeting said, "Those opposed?"

Even I could tell there weren't as many hands in the air this time. I snuck a glance at Mr. Goodwin, thinking he'd start yelling again. Instead, his shoulders slumped. He put his hat on, got up, and left the building without saying another word, or even looking at anyone. That made me feel worse than all the yelling and stuff.

Dad quietly said, "Some of the small businesses like his will now have to pay to have their trash hauled away. That's an added expense they may not be able to afford. I'll talk to him."

A shiver ran down my spine. Could *we* afford it?

Packrat, Dad, and I got up to leave, too. But we couldn't get back up the aisle as fast as we'd come down it. People kept stopping me to clap me on the back and tell me what a good kid I was. And that was awesome. But for every two of them was an adult who'd shake their head at me sadly or even glare. Dad kept his hand on my shoulder and stared down those people, especially the couple who looked like they had some bad words to throw my way, like they were doing to Mr. Talbot right now. I glanced back over my shoulder to see a crowd around him, hands waving, voices rising.

Dad put his hand in the middle of my back and gently pushed me forward. "Let's get out of here."

When we arrived home from the town meeting, Dad went right over to Mom in the camp office. She poured him a cup of coffee while he told her all the little details.

"What's done is done," she said, leaning against the coffee counter and taking a sip. "Can't fight city hall!" When Dad gave her a did-you-really-just-say-that look, she sighed. "So we have to move forward and figure out what to do for us. For the camp."

While they were talking, Charlie and his mom came through the store door. My mom started to go over to the register, but the lady stopped her. "No hurry. I need a few groceries, so I'll be a minute." She moved into the grocery aisle. Charlie, though, stopped in front of the postcard rack by the registration counter.

Dad sat down at one of the tables. "We have to find a dumpster service. Fast."

Hearing the word *dumpster,* I looked back at him. "We're not going to recycle?" How weird would that be? The kid who developed the town plan not even recycling himself.

Dad sighed. "Cooper, you know there's no way we're going to get every single camper that comes through here to sort their trash. We've always picked it up from the campsites and hauled it away for them. It's a customer-service thing they're used to."

"Maybe over time, we can get them to do it," Mom said.

"But not right away," Dad continued. "Just having to take their own trash to the dumpster is going to make some of our customers as frustrated as you saw those people at town meeting today."

Packrat nudged me. I'd almost forgotten he was there. "Go on," he urged. "Tell him what you told me."

Dad tipped his head to one side, in a what's-up kind of way. I took a deep breath. "I've been thinking. What if we set up our own recycling station right here?" When Dad started to shake his head, I said quickly, "Next to a dumpster. Like the transfer station is gonna do, but smaller. Campers who want to can sort their own trash into clear bags. This way, the dumpster won't fill up as fast, and maybe we won't have to pay to have it emptied as often."

"What do we recycle?" Mom grabbed the coffeepot to refill her and Dad's mugs.

"Paper and plastics—" I began.

"Tin and glass," Packrat continued.

"Cardboard." The sides of Dad's mouth curled up a little.

I smiled back. "Those are the big ones."

The lady came out of the grocery aisle with a box of macaroni and cheese and a can of green beans. "When you get a minute, I'm ready to check out," she said.

Mom smiled. "Coming, Lynn." To us, she said, "I'll get started on calling dumpster companies and see what they're charging."

Dad stood to put his and Mom's coffee cups by the little sink.

"What's next?" Packrat asked him.

"I'll go around and tell the seasonal campers. We have to start this immediately." He shook his head and muttered, "What the heck is Talbot thinking? There's no warning at all. No time to prepare. But . . ." He clapped a hand on my shoulder and smiled down. "I like your recycling station idea, Cooper. I think it just might do the trick."

As Packrat and I made our way through the store, I saw Dad stop at the counter. "Don't sign up for a dumpster service yet; just get the prices," he said. "We have to plan for the additional cost. Between that and the gas to transport the recycling to the center, not to mention my time away from other camp projects—"

"I know," Mom said, handing Lynn her bag of groceries. "It's always something around here, isn't it?"

Watching the Connors go out the front door, I thought, *It sure is.*

I hadn't seen Mom ring up a wooden loon on the register with Lynn's food, but I was pretty sure I'd just seen Charlie stuffing one in his pocket while he held the door for his mom.

Chapter 7

Male black bears do not help raise their cubs.

As Packrat and I locked up the pool for the night, and checked the bathrooms to make sure they had toilet paper in every stall, I kept thinking about Charlie stuffing that little loon statue into his pocket. I wished I'd said something like, "Oh, did you forget to pay for that?" Or "Doesn't that wooden loon look real?" Anything so my mom and his mom would know he had it. But I didn't know how to mention it without sounding like a snitch or a tattletale. Or worse, a brat. 'Cause the truth was, it made me mad that he'd stolen from our store. I knew my parents had to pay for the stuff that went into it. So it was like stealing from them. Or me.

"I don't know what I woulda done if I'd seen him take it." Packrat was holding a men's-room stall open with one foot, so he could talk to me as I cleaned the sinks. Sliding a roll of toilet paper in the dispenser, he asked, "Is it too late to tell your mom now?"

I looked at him in the mirror over the sink. "Kinda. I mean, it's my word against his, right?"

Packrat shrugged. "I guess. Are you sure he took it? A hundred percent?"

I had to admit it. "No."

"We'll just have to watch. See if he does it again."

My radio crackled. "Coop?"

I pulled it off my pocket to answer. "Almost done."

"Great! Would you and Packrat like to start the campfire tonight?" asked my mom.

Packrat grinned and gave me a thumbs-up. "Sure!" I told her. "Be right there!"

By the time we'd stacked thin pieces of wood into a tepee-shaped pile in the metal fire ring, Dad had arrived. Packrat took a round, wax fire starter from one of his vest pockets and slid it under the pieces of wood. From another pocket, he took a long-handled lighter to light the top of it.

The three of us stood around the ring. Flames licked at the little slivers of wood, once, twice, three and four times, before getting a tiny bit bigger and catching hold. Higher and higher the flames went, eating away at the wood.

Through the store windows, I saw Mom sweeping the floor and doing all the little things you have to do to close up. I knew she'd be out to join us soon. Molly came skipping off the playground to stand beside Dad and lean up against him. She swiped at her eyes with the back of her hand.

"What's the matter?" Dad asked.

"I fell off the swing." Molly was trying hard not to break down and cry.

"Are you okay?" Dad brushed some sand off her knees.

"Yeah." Molly nodded a bunch of times, making her ponytail bob. "Charlie helped me."

Dad swooped her up and set her in his lap. "I like that young man," he said.

My sister wrapped her arms around Dad's neck, laying her head on his shoulder. "He says he lives here now. They don't have a house."

Dad rubbed her shoulder. "They fell on some hard times and lost their farm."

Molly sat straight up. "They lost it? People lose their houses?" Eyes wide, she whispered, "Could we lose the campground?"

The crackling of the campfire was the only sound for a minute or two. I could tell Dad wanted to be honest, but not worry Molly too much. "If your mom and I couldn't pay the bank what we owe, then yes. There are lots of reasons people lose their homes and businesses.

In Lynn's case, it was because she couldn't make enough from the farm to pay for it." He hugged Molly. "But they're here now, and the campground will be their home for a bit."

"But . . ." Packrat and I caught each other's eye and I knew, like me, that he was thinking of Lynn and Charlie living in their little tent. "We close in October."

Dad looked at me. "Lynn hopes to find a place to work and live by then. We'll do what we can to help them get back on their feet."

Packrat threw a log on the fire, then moved it around with a metal poker until it was in the hottest spot.

Pop-pop-pop. Car tires crunching on our dirt driveway broke into my thoughts. Everyone turned to watch a car roll through the gate. Headlights shone on us for a second, until the car turned, slowed, and parked. Once the headlights went out, I could see it was not a car but a familiar green pickup truck with the Maine Warden Service logo on the driver side door. Game Warden Kate.

Warden Kate's truck door opened and closed. She waved at us. "Nice night like this, I knew you'd have a fire. I'll just grab a cup of coffee, if you don't mind. Be right there."

Another set of tires *pop-pop-popped* on the driveway, coming to a stop behind her truck.

Warden Kate turned back with a smile. The car's passenger door opened, and a light went on inside. Roy!

Campfire forgotten, Packrat and I jumped up and raced to see him.

" 'Bout time!" I called.

"Still like snow days?" Packrat teased.

Roy wasn't smiling. Nor was his father.

Uh-oh.

Roy went to open the back door of the car. His dad tried to help, but Roy stepped in his way. He hauled his oversize backpack from the car, swinging it back so hard that it hit his father in the knee.

"Hey!" yelled his dad. Mr. Parker bent down, one hand on the car, and the other on his knee. I swear I saw a tear in his eye. In a quieter voice, he said, "I told you, I'm sorry. I didn't plan this."

Roy shrugged. "Whatever."

He turned to my dad, who'd come up behind me. "We were supposed to open the camper," Roy said, shooting his father a look that had me feeling a little bad for his dad. I'd been on the wrong side of that look before. It wasn't fun. "But he's gotta go right back, and my mom can't come up until tomorrow night after work. Can I hang out with Cooper for tonight?"

Roy's dad limped toward my dad. "Sorry about this, Jim. We were already practically here when I got the call from my office. A major client needs an emergency meeting first thing in the morning, and I have to prepare. I brought nothing with me."

Dad clapped him on the back. "Roy is welcome anytime, Mike. I trust you know that."

Behind us, the lights in the store went out. Warden Kate came out onto the porch, a mug in her hand. She looked back at Mom, who was locking the door.

Dad tipped his head toward the campfire. "Stay for a few minutes? I can put on more coffee."

Roy's dad looked at his watch. He sighed. "Wish I could. I have to stop by the office and grab a few things, make a few notes." He glanced down at Roy, and even I could tell his eyes were full of an unspoken *I'm sorry.* "Life of a lawyer, you know."

Roy shot his father another of his I-don't-care looks.

"I'll be back as soon as I can," Mr. Parker said. He slid into the driver's seat, his mind already on whatever it was he had to get back to.

Chapter 8

A black bear will give birth to two to four blind and helpless cubs in January during hibernation.

Before his father's car had even rolled out past the gate, Roy had picked up his backpack and headed for my tent, which was set up on the front lawn. Packrat and I watched him toss the pack inside. When he turned to walk back with us, he put his hands in his pockets, hunched his shoulders, and kicked a pebble.

"Hey!" Packrat's voice was a little too happy. He opened his vest to pull out a bag of marshmallows from a left inside pocket. He tossed the bag at Roy, who caught it.

"Bet you don't have Reese's peanut butter cups in there," he mumbled.

Packrat reached into a right inside pocket, and pulled out a handful of Roy's favorite chocolate. "You lose!"

Roy stood a little straighter now, a smile cracking upward. "*You* lose! Those are bite-size! Not s'more-size."

Packrat gave Roy a little shove. "You didn't say what size they had to be! Did he, Cooper?"

I laughed. "Nope."

Roy gave *me* a little shove, then stole a chocolate from Packrat's hand before he could pull them away. Unwrapping it, he tossed it up in the air and caught it in his mouth. "I'll need three or four on each s'more to make it work," he warned.

Roy was officially back.

We stepped into the fire circle and sat on a bench. Packrat's mom, Stacey, and a few more people had joined the campfire while we were away. Warden Kate was leaning forward in her chair, talking across the fire to Mom and Dad. "So, no luck at all?" she asked.

Mom shook her head. "I called all the dumpster services. The only one for this area is Mainely Trash."

Dad gave a bark of a laugh. "One service! And what they charge is highway robbery. Ridiculous!"

Packrat's mom asked, "What about the name of the one up by us, in Weld?"

"They won't come all the way here," Mom said quietly. "Wish they would, though; they're half the price."

Warden Kate frowned. "And the one I gave you?"

Mom shook her head.

Packrat slid three marshmallows onto a roasting stick and held them over the red-hot coals while Roy starting unwrapping the chocolates.

Molly called out to us from the other side of the fire. "Can we have a s'more too?"

We? For the first time, I noticed Charlie sitting next to her. He must have come over while we were putting Roy's stuff in my tent.

"I'll need more graham crackers," Packrat answered.

"There are some in the house," Mom said. "Go get them, Molly." Turning to Dad, she asked, "Are you sure we can't load our dump truck and drive the trash to the incinerator ourselves?"

Even from across the campfire, I could see the frown on Dad's face. "The cost of gas and the time to drive down there and back, plus the extra person I'd have to hire to make sure the usual jobs and chores got done around here . . . I imagine it'd cost almost as much as the dumpster service." He paused. "The whole thing really messes up our routine here. And for a lot of other businesses, too. This dumpster service knows it. They know they're the only game in town; that's why they're charging so much. That's why they'll get away with it."

Dad gave me a small smile. "Good news is, we probably won't be able to afford that new pool liner this year."

Mom frowned. "And why is that good news?"

Packrat, Roy, and I laughed. We knew why. " 'Cause on the really hot days," I explained, "when we're working, Dad sends us pool-diving to patch the leaks."

Mom rolled her eyes, but in a fun way. "So you get paid to go swimming."

"Something like that," Dad said, chuckling.

Seeing the marshmallows drooping from Packrat's stick, I said, "Hey! You're gonna lose them in the fire!"

Molly returned and sat next to Packrat, setting down a package of graham crackers and bars of chocolate. "Come get a s'more," she said to Charlie. She took out a graham cracker square and held it out to him.

Charlie shook his head. "No, thank you."

Molly stared him down. "Why not?"

"I'm not hungry."

Putting her hands on her hips, she said, "Nobody ever *doesn't* want a s'more!"

I leaned over to tell her to leave him alone. If he didn't want one, he didn't want one. But before I could, Charlie blurted, "What's a s'more?"

Everyone gasped. Then we burst out laughing. Charlie half stood up, looking around the circle at all of us like he was going to bolt. Dad put a hand on his arm. I said quickly, "Sorry! We're not laughing at you."

Roy shook his head. "We just can't believe you've never had one!"

"Check this out," Packrat instructed him. Charlie watched as he put a square of chocolate onto the graham cracker square, then slid a melted, golden-brown marshmallow on top. Then he topped it all with another graham cracker. "A s'more!" Packrat said, handing it to him.

Even the adults watched as Charlie slowly took his first bite. His left eyebrow went up, then the right. His eyes shone. He quickly took a second bite. A third bite, and the s'more was gone.

"Those are awesome!" he exclaimed.

"It's the chocolate," Molly said. "It gets all melty on the hot marsh-mallow. Want another?"

"Yes, please!"

Game Warden Kate took a sip of coffee and turned to me. "Your mom showed me the blue flask bottle and the tiger lilies, Cooper," she said. Her eyes twinkled at me over her coffee mug. "Nicely done."

Dad shot me a teasing look. "I saw them, too. What'd you do?"

I froze for a second, sending Packrat a panicked look. "What do you mean, what'd I do?" I was stalling for time. I had to think. Had he found the broken coffee mug in the trash? Did he know about the whole package of Twinkies that Packrat and I had taken from the kitchen and eaten in our kayaks yesterday?

Dad threw another log on the fire. He raised an eyebrow at me before putting on a second.

"Umm, I didn't do anything. I just found the bottle and saw the flowers, and they made me think of Mom." I tried to make my face look innocent.

Mom gave me an isn't-he-so-thoughtful smile.

Dad half-laughed, half-coughed and gave me an I-taught-you-well-son look.

Roy shifted in his seat. For just a second, when he glanced at me, I thought I saw a flash of anger. But when I looked back, he was smiling.

Game Warden Kate chuckled quietly. "Well, I for one prefer wild-flowers over store-bought ones." I decided to save that information in case I ever needed a favor or something. She pointed at me, asking, "But that bottle. It's gorgeous. Where did you get it?"

"We'd seen a . . ."—I was about to say "bear," but seeing Mom's curious face across the fire, I changed my mind—". . . wildlife trail, and followed that until I saw the first bottle sticking out of the ground. That led to Packrat finding an old cellar hole."

Roy groaned. "Trails! Cellar hole? Again, I miss out!"

"We'll take you," Packrat said quickly. "There are more bottles there, all buried like someone threw them there a long time ago."

"A bottle dump," Warden Kate said.

Packrat nodded. "And we found a w—"

I side-kicked him in the shin. "A wall," he finished. "And a huge, old, falling-down fireplace."

"A wall? Fireplace?" Mom's radar switched on. No way was I telling her there was a hand-dug well that was more than ten feet deep there. She'd never let me go back until it was filled in. And probably not for a hundred years after that. "Do you know where he's talking about, Kate?" she asked.

"Is it at the north end of the lake?" When I nodded, she said, "I do. It's the site of an old inn on the stagecoach run. Lots of history there. But your bottle . . ."

"My bottle?"

"It's old. Really old. Probably a hundred and fifty years old."

Everyone went quiet. All we heard was the crackle and creaks of the campfire, as the flames danced around the wood.

"It's probably worth at least a hundred and forty dollars," she said.

Mom gasped. Packrat and I looked at each other in amazement.

"Did you say *a hundred and forty* dollars?" Roy exclaimed. "For an old bottle?"

"One bottle?" Charlie breathed.

"That," Game Warden Kate confirmed, "and maybe more."

Chapter 9

Bears are not considered true hibernators (animals who lower their body temperatures almost to freezing), but they do spend most of the winter asleep in their den. The dens can be a space they dig out in a hillside, under a rock or bit of ledge, under the exposed root system of a tree, or inside a hollow tree.

Roy gave a low whistle. "One hundred and forty dollars." He'd said this, like, three times since Warden Kate had told us how much she thought the light blue bottle was worth.

"Sounds like you definitely found an old bottle dump," she said. "Back in those days, when a house or business had glass it didn't want, they found a natural hole or banking and threw it there, separate from other trash. The fact that the bottle survived all these years, isn't broken, and that it's blue, makes it worth something." She grinned. "I know many a collector who'd love to have found that bottle."

I grinned back at her. That was pretty cool.

"So there's more?" Charlie took a step toward me. "Bottles?"

"I think so," I said. "But I'm not sure what shape they're in."

"Charlie?" Lynn stepped into the circle. "There you are. I thought I heard your voice."

Molly piped up. "I invited him over for s'mores. 'Cause he helped me when I fell earlier."

Lynn smiled. "That was awfully sweet of you. But he was supposed to be back at the site half an hour ago." She looked at her son. "I was getting worried!"

Charlie looked like he wanted to crawl in a hole. I knew that feeling. My own mom was one of the biggest worrywarts I knew. I figured he wasn't seven, like Molly, but he wasn't quite as old as us, either.

"I'll walk you back," his mom said.

Shrugging off her hand on his arm, he turned to look straight at me. "Could you take me sometime? Bottle digging?"

I hesitated. He'd caught me by surprise. I wasn't sure I wanted a little kid tagging along with me and my friends. And then, there was what I was pretty sure I'd seen—him taking the loon statue and all. Could I trust him?

"Where exactly is this spot?" Dad threw another log on the fire.

"I was wondering that myself," Stacey said, shooting my dad a grateful look.

So while the campfire crackled, I explained how Packrat and I had been watching the turtle fight, which had Roy groaning and throwing his hands in the air because once again, he'd missed something cool. I told which cove it was, how we'd spotted the animal trail between the two rocks, and then walked straight back into the woods from there.

I did not, repeat *not*, mention the adult bear print.

"Yep," Dad said. "That's our land. It's a small, skinny piece in the very back corner between the lake and Pine Road."

Lynn frowned. "Charlie, I don't think it's a good idea, you being out on the lake or over at the bottle dump without an adult. Without me."

"C'mon, Mom! I kayaked downriver before with Dad, before he . . . well, he . . ."

Lynn gave her son a sad look. "Not without me. That's final." She turned my way. "No offense to you, Cooper. I just couldn't bear to have anything happen."

She led him away, saying something about him not being old enough to go off like that. And he was going to have boundaries while they stayed here. Or there'd be consequences.

Charlie looked back at me over his shoulder, and I gave him a sympathetic look.

Mom's voice brought me back to the campfire. "Jim, did you know this cellar hole was there? That it was an inn?"

Dad shook his head, and looked at Warden Kate.

Roy's shoulder bumped mine, then he leaned in on my left to whisper, "So the bottle's yours."

Packrat leaned in on my right. "When do we go back?"

"Tomorrow?" I whispered back. "Packrat, come camp out with Roy and me. We'll go online and see what we need for tools to dig them up." I wasn't sure which crackled louder, the wood on the fire, or our excitement over the bottle dump.

"I'll go get my sleeping bag," Packrat said, standing up.

"I could use the walk," Roy said, as my two friends stepped from the campfire light into the darkness. I was standing up to follow when I heard Warden Kate say, "—about two hundred years old."

I sat back down. "What's two hundred years old?"

"The Wayside Inn," she said. "That was the name of it. If you like history, the inn has a ton of it. This town, and the lake, used to be quite a summer tourist spot. Next time you boys are over there, by the cellar hole, see if you can find the stairs that go nowhere."

My mother rolled her eyes. "Now you've gone and done it. We'll never keep him home to work!" Dad and Warden Kate laughed. But Mom was right. I was itching to get back there.

Warden Kate pushed back a lock of hair from her face and tucked it behind her ear. "There are tons of local legends around the inn. Back then, it was right on the stagecoach road, with the lake behind it. A very pretty spot—not a lot of trees then, so it had great views. People used to go there to escape the city when it got hot in the summer. At least one president stopped there for lunch on his way up north. They claimed some very famous people stayed for weekends, and for longer visits, as well."

"And the stairs that go nowhere?" I asked.

"People think they were built up to a wooden gazebo, where the guests would gather to look at the lake. Or, some people think they led to a small house for guests, or the groundskeeper."

Seeing two shadows come back to stand just outside the light of the campfire, I got up to join them. "Cooper?" Mom called softly.

I turned back to her. She crooked her finger and I went to crouch down next to her. "Yeah?"

"Remember, you have to rake the playground in the morning."

"Okay." I started to stand, but she tugged on my shirt until I bent down over her shoulder so she could kiss my cheek.

"Thank you again for the flowers. You made my day brighter with your beautiful gift."

I rolled my eyes and mumbled something like "Yeah, whatever." But as soon as I walked into the darkness outside the fire circle, I couldn't help but smile.

Until I saw Roy flash me that annoyed look again.

What the heck did I do?

Nights in mid-June can be warm enough for shorts and a T-shirt. But this was not one of those nights. It was about 40 degrees, and we were all sitting inside our sleeping bags, long pants and sweatshirts on. I had my laptop on my lap. Packrat and Roy had their tablets out. We didn't say much as we searched for information on old bottles and bottle dumps.

Roy seemed quieter than usual. Like before, his annoyed look disappeared faster than it had appeared. Maybe it wasn't me he was mad at.

"I can't find a bottle exactly like the one I gave Mom," I told them. "But I found one kind of like it. What did Warden Kate call it? A flask? This one, here, is a hundred and fifty dollars."

Grrrgh. Grrrgh.

"What was that?" I put my laptop down beside me, and crawled to the tent flap to look outside.

"Sooorrry," Roy mumbled. I turned back to stare at him.

"That was *you?*" Packrat's eyebrows shot up as high as they could go. "Seriously! I thought a bear was out there! Here," he said, reaching into a long, skinny vest pocket. He pulled out a snack-size package. "Have some cookies."

Roy held one hand to his stomach and reached out for the cookies with the other. But he dropped them into his lap unopened and went back to his tablet.

Wait, what? He wasn't wolfing them down? Something was horribly wrong.

"What's up?" I asked gently.

"You wouldn't understand," he said, not even looking up.

"Try us," Packrat coaxed.

Roy picked up the cookie package and dropped it again. "I was so mad at Dad, that when he asked if I wanted to stop for supper, I said no." His stomach rumbled again. "I didn't want to have to stare at him over burgers."

I felt bad for Roy. I really did. I thought my dad worked a lot. But at least he was here in the campground with me. I could go find him and spend five minutes with him whenever I wanted. But Roy's dad worked from his office. And the way Roy talked, he worked days, nights, and weekends, too. Just like my dad. Except Roy's dad wasn't around when he did it.

"Even Mom was pretty mad this time." Roy ducked his head.

Packrat's and my eyes met over our friend's shoulder. Roy never, ever, ever shared family stuff.

Packrat prompted him. "She was?"

"Uh-huh. She said it was the last straw." Roy looked at us both. "What's she mean by that?"

Now my stomach felt all twisted. I think he knew, but he was kind of hoping for us to tell him everything was going to be all right.

"It means," began Packrat slowly, "that he's done it too many times for her. As in, the straw that broke the camel's back."

"Oh." Roy's voice was so small, I wasn't sure I'd heard it over the chirping of the crickets outside. He went back to swiping pages and looking at bottles.

I guess the conversation was done.

"Hey!" Roy's yell practically had me jumping out of my sleeping bag. He slid his tablet across to me. "I found something!"

Packrat wiggled himself and his sleeping bag over to Roy's other side. The website on his screen was called Bottle Digger Adventures.

"Read it," Roy urged. I wasn't quite sure if he really wanted me to read it, or if he just wanted to take us off the subject of his parents.

Didn't matter. I read:

> Bottle dumps are a type of archaeology. By digging up a bottle dump, you can learn a lot about a family from the 1700s. Not wanting their trash too close to the house, they tended to sort it, and then dump it, in a chosen spot. During that time period, not much was thrown away, so it took years for the dump to grow. Usually, they chose a low spot, a hole of sorts, or a banking, that was away from the house.

"The one you found was on a banking," Packrat reminded me. "Near the inn."

*Amber-colored bottles are traditionally very old. Many
bottle diggers are very secretive, because old bottles, in
excellent shape, can be sold for a great deal of money.
One bottle that was made to hold a rare mineral sold for
$17,000.*

"What?" Roy cried.

"Whoa!" Packrat exclaimed. "That'd be enough to cover the dumpster company's fees, no problem!"

Yep. It would.

But it also might help a homeless family get back on their feet.

Chapter 10

The home range of a male black bear is several times larger than a female's, which is six to nineteen square miles. A young bear has a range of only four to eight square miles.

The next morning, Roy and Packrat were snoring so loudly, I was surprised the tent didn't take off like a hot air balloon. No way was I going to be able to fall back asleep, even if I wanted to. So I slid on my sneakers and went in to the house to grab some breakfast. I tried to open the door quietly, but I saw right away that I didn't need to. Dad was already up, sitting at the kitchen counter, telling Mom how he'd been up all night, thinking about the trash situation. He'd decided to call Mainely Trash to come out, look things over, and give him a price. The guy who answered the phone said all his employees were already swamped with people who needed dumpsters. If Dad wanted to have his trash taken away, he had to come into town to see *them*.

Let's just say Dad was about as happy as a mountain lion that'd fallen in the water. Most salesmen came to him because they wanted to see exactly what we needed, where we might put it, or to measure something. And because it was good customer service.

With the town transfer station closing to local businesses in a week, we sure did need that dumpster. So even though Dad had tons of things he should have been doing, he had to go. That left me: vacuuming the pool, which meant I ended up starting all my other jobs that much later; cleaning the bathrooms; raking the playground; raking the campsites; and watering the flowers. Luckily for me, Packrat and Roy grabbed a couple of rakes to help me, so we could get out on the lake sooner and get over to the bottle dump.

Cooper and Packrat: Mystery of the Bear Cub

Finally, I only had watering the flowers left on my list. And it wasn't just a couple of pots on the ground. Oh, no. My mom planted a gazillion of them all over the place, and hung a trillion more. Okay, maybe not quite that many, but when you had to water them, it sure felt like it. There were at least a dozen pots of petunias in every color imaginable at the pool, another eight ground pots decorating the entrance, and there were three beds of flowers in every height, color, and size. When Mom wasn't looking, I'd drag out a big old watering hose, and spray as far as I could before moving it to the next spigot. But Mom didn't like that, because if you didn't do it just right, the rushing water beat down the blossoms and hurt the roots. I was supposed to lug a five-gallon watering can—pink, with yellow flowers on it.

Not exactly the manliest of jobs.

I always left the biggest garden with the little pond for last. That's because my three-legged frog Oscar lived there. As I watered, he always swam over to the edge of the pond to watch. Today, though, he'd climbed out on a rock to sit. I smiled to see him there. "You found yourself a sunny spot—"

"Hi, Cooper," came a voice from behind me. I turned to look, and there was Charlie walking by with his mom.

"Hi—" I began, but his mother had one hand on his arm and was speed-walking by.

"Mom! Look! It's a three-legged frog—" he started, but she wasn't paying him any mind. Before I knew it, they were turning the corner to the store.

Molly came up next to me. "His mom won't let him play today. I think he's in trouble."

My radio crackled. "Cooper?" Mom asked, although she had to have known it'd be me. "Almost done with the watering?"

"Yep." Seeing Roy and Packrat hanging up their rakes, I smiled. Time to head to the bottle dump.

"Dad's back. He wants you to come by the office as soon as you're done, okay?"

I groaned. But not with my finger on the ON button.

Together, my friends, Molly, and I walked to the store. Dad was waiting on the porch.

"Sorry, boys. I know your work shift is almost done, but the dumpster company needs us to clear, level, and put stone dust on the exact spot where we'll be putting the dumpster. They usually do that, but they're so backed up with new customers, they said they wouldn't sign us up unless we took care of it ourselves."

"So they're coming today?" I asked.

"They couldn't give me an exact day. Or even a week," Dad said with a sigh.

"Awww, Dad, do we have to do all of it today? I mean, we were gonna go—"

"Hey!" Roy's voice was so sharp, Molly moved behind me. Roy pointed to my dad, but he stared me down. "If your dad needs us, we stay!"

Just then, Mom came rushing out the door. Seeing Dad, her mouth lifted in one of the biggest smiles I'd ever seen. "Jim! You have to come hear this!" And she rushed back into the store.

"Your mom is up to something," Dad muttered as we all followed her inside. Packrat and I hung back to exchange a look behind Roy's back.

"What was *that* all about?" I muttered. "I was just asking if it could wait a day."

Packrat shrugged. "Got me."

Mom talked as she walked back behind the counter. "Lynn, you remember my husband, Jim." Mom seemed so excited, she was practically hopping up and down. I didn't get it; it was just Lynn and Charlie. I didn't think they were famous or anything, like the King family, who'd camped with us last summer while taping their *Open Road* reality show.

"So, Lynn has an idea on how to help us with our trash problem." Mom giggled. "I mean, well, we don't have a trash *problem*. But the hauling away of the trash." Mom waved a hand in the air. "Jim! They want to haul our trash to the transfer station for half the cost of the dumpster service!"

Dad lifted his hat and scratched his head, looking at Lynn the whole time. Setting it back on his head, he finally spoke. "Okay. Tell me about it—your service. Tell me how you'll do it."

"You remember the old diesel pickup truck I arrived in?" Lynn began. "It's one of the few things I still have from our farm. It has a one-ton dump body, and my dad took real good care of it."

For a second, I thought that if Dad were to say the truck could never haul stuff, Lynn would have a thing or two to say back at him. Her gaze fell to Charlie, then back to my dad.

"We were in the Post Office, signing up to get our mail delivered here, when I heard about the problem you're having, about how all the businesses around here are in trouble with the new transfer station rules. And I heard how you were all being taken for a ride by Mainely Trash and . . . well . . ."

She paused and cleared her throat. "I ran our farm side by side with my parents," she said. "I'd still be there now if their hospital bills hadn't made me sell off everything we held dear. Including the farm itself."

Lynn stopped talking. The store was so quiet, we could've heard a mouse squeak. She cleared her throat again. "I know how to work hard from sunup to sundown. Feeding cows, chickens, making breads, jellies, planting crops. And all the while taking care of my elderly parents. Charlie, too." She looked my dad in the eye. "Hauling your trash will be nothing compared to that. I need work to feed my son and to pay you for our campsite."

I glanced at Charlie. He was looking up at his mom, and I swear he was holding his breath.

"Daddy?" Molly loud-whispered. She pulled on Dad's shirt until he looked down at her. "I want them to stay."

Dad stared out the window for a minute. Finally, he said, "Lynn, you're in no way prepared for the trash you'd have to haul away from here twice a week."

For a minute, I thought Mom was going to fly over the counter. "Did you not hear what she just said?"

Dad held up a hand and gave her his just-hold-on-a-minute-'cause-I'm-not-done look. To Lynn, he said, "You'll need to build sides on the dump body to hold all the bags in securely. You'll need to cover it with a tarp so nothing flies off your load. It's a long haul to the incinerator . . ."

As Dad talked, you could see both Lynn's and Charlie's shoulders square up as if they were getting ready to load the trash right this minute. In my mind, I imagined them doing fist pumps in the air, but you didn't see any of that on their faces.

"I'll help build the sides." Dad was still figuring things out. "But you have to talk to the incinerator plant ahead of time to see what you need and what's expected—"

"Already done." Lynn lifted her chin, as if she expected Dad might not believe her. "We're good to go. We just needed a customer."

Dad glanced at Mom with a raised eyebrow.

Mom flashed him a smile.

"Okay," he said. "But I'm serious about the amount of trash you'll be hauling out of here when all hundred and thirty-two sites are full of campers in a couple of weeks. I figure you'll have a very, very big load with no room for more, on Mondays and Fridays."

Lynn put her arm around Charlie's shoulder. "Mondays and Fridays, it is. Your wife said you used to drive around and pick up the trash on each campsite? We can do that for you, too, then take the load to the station." She paused to look at Charlie, who nodded encouragingly. "That'd cost a little more, though."

Dad grinned. "Of course it will. It should. How about—"

Mom interrupted. "I've been thinking about that," she said. She ignored Dad's look this time. "I have a rental trailer that is open for the whole summer. What if we have you two stay there, instead of in your tent, in trade for the on-site trash pickup?"

For a second, Lynn got a really weird look on her face. Like she had something stuck in her eye or something. Charlie leaned in to her. "Mom? Please?"

Hesitating only a second, she took a step closer to Dad and held out her hand. "I'm glad we can help each other out."

Dad shook it.

"Charlie will help me," Lynn said, turning to Mom. "And I promise, there will be no more trouble from him in your store."

Mom nodded slightly. "Charlie, I really appreciate you coming in and being honest."

For the first time, I noticed the wooden loon on the counter between them. I stared from Mom to Charlie and back again.

Lynn raised an eyebrow at Charlie, but to Mom, she said, "I know how we would have felt if someone had stolen one of my jars of home-made jam from our farm store."

"Sorry, Mrs. Wilder." Charlie shuffled his feet back and forth. "I . . . I just wanted to get my mom a birthday present. But every time I tried to wrap it, my stomach hurt."

"He'll be with me every second from now on," Lynn assured us.

"No need." Mom smiled. "He told the truth. And besides, we believe in second chances around here." And she handed her the key to Rental 116.

Chapter 11

From the late 1800s to the early 1900s, open garbage dumps became the sites of Garbage Dump Bear Shows. Even Yellowstone National Park dumped food trash to attract bears for tourists.

For the next four days, it rained. Not a light rain, either. Sprinkling wouldn't have stopped us from taking Roy to see the cellar hole. Heck, rainy days were good fishing days, and we could have dropped a line in the water on the way. But a blustery wind that made the rain fall sideways instead of straight down? That kept us close to home.

It didn't stop us from having to work, though, because there are always jobs to be done in a campground, no matter the weather. We cleaned bathrooms, helped Roy's mother set up her camper for the season, and swept the store porch. We wiped down the laundry room and we hauled wood. And we bailed boats a gazillion times.

But the next morning, Roy came rushing through the store's screen door with a hopeful smile on his face.

"It's letting up! Let's go!" he said. He held the door open and pointed up. "I even see a patch of blue sky!"

"It's more like an itty bitty speck." Packrat stepped in behind him and shook his head sadly. Still, he gave me a hopeful look.

"Can't," I said, even though I'd had the same idea just minutes before. "Mom told me there's a thunderstorm warning till noon."

Packrat and Roy groaned. "I'll never get to see the cellar hole!" Roy exclaimed.

Dad stepped out of the camp office and looked at our long faces. "Mr. Goodwin called," he said. "Our doughnut order is ready. He's even got them wrapped and priced."

"Just in time," Mom said. "I sold the last one this morning."

Dad squeezed my shoulder. "Want to come along for the ride, Cooper?"

Mom shook her head. "I don't think that's such a good idea."

"What? Why?" I cried. Mr. Goodwin had the best homemade doughnuts around. And if today was his baking day, I might score a warm chocolate one, with extra powdered sugar.

"Because I want my doughnut order to make it home. All seventy-two of them!"

Dad and I laughed, while Mom gave me a warm smile over the registration counter. She arranged her flowers in the blue bottle again.

A prickly feeling hit me between the shoulders, and the hair on the back of my neck stood up. Looking around, I noticed Roy talking behind his hand to Packrat. His eyes made contact with mine, but I didn't feel like he was laughing with me. More like he was laughing at me. Packrat wouldn't even look my way.

"If you can trust us," Dad was still teasing Mom, "I'll take all three amigos. They've earned a treat, working in the rain these last few days."

"I'll be counting those doughnuts when you get back!" Mom called after us as we left.

Roy kind of power-walked the last few yards to the camp dump truck and went right for the passenger-door handle. I stopped dead in my tracks like a squirrel that's seen a coyote up ahead. That was my seat. I rode shotgun in Dad's truck. Always.

Roy shot me a triumphant look as he opened the door and climbed in. Packrat tugged on my sleeve. "Let it go, Coop."

"What'd he say back there?" I asked.

Packrat shook his head, and opened the door to the backseat. "Ask him yourself, okay? I don't want to be in the middle of it."

The middle of what? I had no idea what was up with Roy.

It wasn't a long ride, maybe a mile on our dirt driveway. After that, it was another three miles down the road until we hit the edge of Main

Street. This was where all the town action happened. Well, as much action as you could have in the country. Every time we drove through, my dad had this little joke he'd say: "Don't blink, Cooper! You'll miss it!"

We drove past the library on our right, then our school. Another half-mile and we passed the town hall on the left, where we'd had the meeting that'd started this whole mess. At that point, the road split into a kind of rotary, only it wasn't round. More like a really, really long oval. The middle was a raised grassy area, with benches and a square memorial stone with our founding fathers' names engraved on it. At the top of that was a colonial soldier in uniform.

On the right side of the oval were six big old houses in a row with barns and pretty yards. On the left side was a white church with a tall steeple, the post office, and then Mr. Goodwin's General Store.

Dad parked out front of Mr. Goodwin's and we all scrambled out of his pickup truck. When we opened the front door to his store, a bell, hanging from the top of the door, tinkled our arrival.

Mr. Goodwin's store wasn't fancy, but it was clean and comfortable. There were signs from what he called the Good Ol' Days all over the walls. Rows of groceries, snacks, candy, and toiletries lined the back. In the front was a long, old-fashioned eating counter with stools; they were attached to the floor, but you could still spin on them.

Mr. Goodwin wiped his hands on a towel and came over to greet us. "Here for your order?" he asked.

Dad nodded and sat on one of the stools. "And four more to eat here." Roy sat on one side of him and I sat on the other. Packrat took the stool next to me.

Mr. Goodwin lifted a plate of chocolate doughnuts from the top of the warm pizza oven, and put it down in front of us. "Figured you might all come," he said with a wink at me.

Leaning up against his counter, he said to Dad, "So, I suppose you heard the news. That dumpster company, they know we businesses have nowhere else to go. They're charging three times the amount they were a week ago. They know they have us over a barrel!"

Packrat snorted, then coughed. I shoved my shoulder into his and frowned. What was he trying to do, make Mr. Goodwin mad?

"Sorry," he mumbled. "It's just . . . over a barrel? Trash?"

Mr. Goodwin's face softened. "No pun intended." Going to the fridge, he pulled out a gallon of milk and poured Packrat a glass. To Dad, he said, "It's happening too fast. Closing the transfer station, having to get dumpsters. Thank goodness the apartment over the store is empty, or I'd have even more trash to deal with!" He poured milk for me and Roy. "Everyone in town is scrambling to figure things out. How will they pay for it? Or will they haul it the two hours to the incinerator themselves? I can't do either of those things."

"Can't?" Dad asked.

"Can't. It's just me running the store right now." Mr. Goodwin sighed heavily. "The dumpster fees could close me down."

Packrat, Roy, and I shared worried glances.

"Business has been slower and slower ever since the big chain stores came in. But my store is still the meeting place for the locals, so I do okay. Till this."

"How long have you had the General Store?" Roy asked.

"Been in my family four generations."

"Wow!" Packrat said.

Mr. Goodwin set the gallon of milk down. "When I was a kid, I insisted I didn't want to take it over from my dad. I was never, ever going to work as hard as he did. Seven days a week. Fifteen-hour days. Opening up before sunrise to have the coffee on for people heading off to work. Breakfast, lunch, supper, selling groceries. Candy sales to the kids after school." His eyes twinkled. "And ice cream to the campground kids in the summer." We laughed with him.

"What changed your mind?" Roy asked. His eyes were intense. "About working with your dad?"

"When I realized he did it for his community." Mr. Goodwin seemed to be trying to find just the right words. "And how much they loved him for it. People came in because they were recognized. They were asked about their day, their kids, their lives."

Just then, the sound of metal falling, rolling, filled the store. But it came from outside, like something had pushed over a mountain of bikes.

Mr. Goodwin looked toward the back door and sighed. "That bear must be back."

A bear? I sucked in a breath, and immediately started coughing on the bits of chocolate doughnut I'd inhaled. *Here?*

Mr. Goodwin was already walking to the back of the store. We jumped up to follow him to look out the back screen door. Pacing the long, skinny parking lot that ran all the way from behind the church down to Mr. Goodwin's store was a black bear. It was about four feet tall, with little eyes, round ears, and a short tail. Its snout was light brown, its fur black.

Seeing Mr. Goodwin's trash cans lying on their sides, I realized we'd heard the bear knocking over his trash cans.

"They're empty," he assured me. "I opened late so I could take the trash to the incinerator at first light. I can't keep that up, though. Not sure what I'm going to do."

We watched the bear trudge around and around the dumpster that stood behind the post office. Giving a grunt, it put its paws halfway up the dumpster and pushed off. Landing on all fours, it grunted again.

Mr. Goodwin shook his head. "All four of the businesses in town feel the way I do. We've gotten together and hired a lawyer, to put a push on Talbot to make things right. But that's going to take time, so we have to figure out a way to get rid of our trash on our own for now."

"Can you all go in together to pay for a dumpster?" Dad asked.

"We're not all in the same area. The post office fills theirs right up, so they don't have room for my trash, too." Mr. Goodwin stood tall. "But honestly, I've decided to make a stand. I'm not paying those prices. They're taking advantage of us!" He lowered his voice and leaned in toward Dad. "Did you know that Mainely Trash is owned by Talbot's cousin?"

The bear was standing on its hind legs again, working its paws under the dumpster cover, looking like it wanted to wiggle up and crawl in.

"We've got to stop them, Jim," said Mr. Goodwin said. "Are you with us?"

Dad cleared his throat. "I know the whole situation stinks. But we found a way to make it work."

"You?" Mr. Goodwin turned to face him. "But you have more trash than all of us combined! How? Who? Wait." He pointed a finger at Dad. "Did you cave? Are you using Mainely—"

Dad held up his hand. "I almost had to. What else could I have done? But then we had an offer from one of our campers. In exchange for a campsite and a paycheck, she'll haul the trash to the transfer station."

I swear, Mr. Goodwin looked like he was going to fall into itty-bitty pieces. Dad put a hand on his shoulder. "Why don't I send Lynn to talk to you?" Dad suggested. "She'll have to charge you a fee, of course, but it won't be as much as Mainely Trash, I can promise you that."

Mr. Goodwin shrugged. "I don't know. Can't hurt to talk to her, at least," he said.

The bear dropped to all fours to walk around the dumpster again. This time it gave three quick grunts in a row, and what sounded like tongue clicks, before getting back up on its hind legs to try to lift the cover again.

"She really wants in today," Mr. Goodwin said. "She doesn't usually work this hard at it."

"She?" I asked.

He scanned the woods across from us. "Yes, she has one cub. It doesn't usually come with her, though. I've only seen it once. I've heard that the moms leave their cubs up in a tree while they forage."

The bear dropped to all fours again with a huff. She gave a double grunt, then a triple grunt, before slowly trudging into the woods.

"Looks like she won't be dumpster-diving today!" Packrat said.

"Ewww!" Roy said. "That's gross! Who knows what's in there? Rotten food . . ."

"Maggots . . . ," I added, relieved to see Roy joining in on the fun.

"Toilet paper!" Packrat wrinkled his nose.

Mr. Goodwin laughed. "In a roundabout way, that reminds me." He looked down with a twinkle in his eye. "Warden Kate told me about the bottle vase you gave your mom."

What was it about that bottle?

"She said you found it on the old Wayside Inn property. I know a little something about that place."

I nodded, wondering what that had to do with dumpster-diving.

"There's an old legend my grandfather used to tell me when I was your age about that inn. It was owned by a man who loved to make money. But he didn't like to spend it much—kind of like me. Back then, the Wayside Inn was on a main road heading north out of the city, and it started to get pretty popular with rich folk."

So far his story was kind of like Warden Kate's.

"He served meals to passersby, and he had a couple of rooms for overnight guests. Eventually he found himself a wife. She was a woman with money of her own, and big plans to make the place grand. She convinced him to add on a couple more rooms. And a year later, a couple more. With the last of her money, the wife insisted on putting in a very fancy, brick-lined, three-hole privy, the likes of which were only seen in the cities—"

"Privy?" asked Roy.

"Think of the tiny closet-size wooden buildings with the half-moon on them," Mr. Goodwin explained.

Packrat added, "Outhouse. Bathroom."

Roy grinned from ear to ear. "Got it."

"With the additions and changes, more and more rich people came, and the money really started flowing in. But the owner? He still refused to spend most of it. His wife became quite angry about it, telling everyone who would listen that he was hoarding it. She wanted to add a boathouse by the water, and a gazebo on the hill. He refused. The wife, she only got a small allowance to make repairs. So she did what she could to maintain the place, but try as she might, she couldn't get him to add on any more improvements. The place started to look old and worn. People stopped coming."

Mr. Goodwin leaned toward us, and lowered his voice. "My grandfather even told me that when the richer travelers paid for their stay or a meal with a rare ten-dollar Liberty gold coin, the owner locked the coins away in a special box. Supposedly, he collected a hundred of them!"

"So what'd he do with all that money?" Packrat asked.

Mr. Goodwin's voice rose a level. "That's the question! The most popular rumor has it that he got so tired of hearing his wife complain and beg for it, he threw the box down her fancy privy one night. He figured one day, when he was ready to use it, he could fish it out. But he knew she wouldn't."

"Ewww!" Roy exclaimed. "Wait. Actually, that's kinda smart."

"Except"—Mr. Goodwin paused to look us all in the eye—"he died before he could dig it out."

Chapter 12

The cry of a newborn human baby can fool a mother bear into retrieving her own cubs.

Once we were back at the campground, Dad looked at the messages on his phone. "I totally forgot. I have to call Stu at Mainely Trash and cancel our contract for the dumpster."

He looked way too happy about that. But who could blame him?

"We just have to make our own recycling center now. That will cut down on the amount of trash Lynn has to haul," he said.

"When did you want to build it?" I asked. *Not now. Not now. Not now,* I prayed.

"Tomorrow." Into the phone he said, "Jim Wilder here. Put Stu on." Putting his hand over the phone, he said to us, "You're all off the clock." Lifting his hand, he listened, then said, "What do you mean, he isn't there? I can hear him talking in the background! Fine. Give him a message for me—"

Dad turned to walk and talk. Packrat, Roy, and I made a break for it. We headed for the lake and our kayaks, laughing, talking, and friendly-shoving all the way. Rounding the last turn in the dirt road, we met Lynn driving up from the lake in her fire-engine-red, oversize pickup truck. On the driver-side door were the words LAKE VIEW FARM. From a distance, the truck looked brand-new. But as she rolled closer, I could see dings, little dents, and small patches of rust here and there. This truck had seen a lot of work, for sure.

We stood off to the side, and Lynn stopped to smile at us through the open driver window. "Figured we'd do a test run to see how long the job will take from here to the incinerator."

I looked past her to see Charlie in the passenger seat. He looked like he wanted to be anywhere but in the truck. I knew from having done this job myself, it was going to be a long day for him. "When my dad and I picked up the trash inside the camp, it was easier for me to stand on the running board when we drove from stop to stop," I suggested. "I just held onto the door and the rearview mirror. That way, I didn't have to open and close the door a million times."

Lynn looked to Charlie, who was giving her a please-please-please look. "Well, I suppose that would be okay. I'm barely driving five miles an hour." As Charlie scrambled out to try it, she winked at me. "Thanks. It'll be more fun for him now."

The three of us turned to watch the truck roll down the road. It swayed from side to side, stopping every fifty feet or so. Lynn and Charlie checked each site's metal trash can. If there was a bag inside, they pulled it out, put it on the ground, tied the top ends together, and swung it up in the air to throw it in the back of the truck bed.

"Remember when we used to do that?" Roy asked.

I laughed as the three of us turned back toward the lake. "You mean, like last week?"

The leaves on the trees were that new-leaf green, swaying slightly in a warm spring breeze. I lifted my face to it, and closed my eyes for a second. It sure felt good to be out of school and the hallways. Spending time in the sun always made me feel like my batteries were getting recharged.

I used my camp keys to get into the boathouse for our life jackets and paddles. Within minutes, I was in my favorite green kayak, Packrat in his blue one, and Roy, in a race-car-red one. Side by side, we paddled for the north end of the lake.

"So how'd you find this old inn place?" Roy asked.

"We found it by accident," I said. "Packrat saw something swim across the lake—"

"I got it on video!"

"And it went into the woods. So we decided to follow it."

Roy playfully threw water with his paddle in our direction. "Couldn't wait for me?"

Packrat gave Roy a sideways glance. "Really? You think Cooper's gonna say, 'Hey, let's not follow a bear we just saw, on a trail we've never hiked before?' "

Roy laughed. "If it were me, I wouldn't wait for him either!" He stopped paddling and turned to us with wide eyes. "Wait. Did you say . . . bear? BEAR!"

Packrat and I looked at each other, then burst out laughing all over again. I'd forgotten Roy hadn't heard that part yet, on account of Mom being at the campfire with us when we'd told the story.

Roy pointed his paddle our way. "Tell me everything. Now."

As we paddled the shoreline, Packrat and I filled in the blanks.

The breeze didn't blow at all on this side of the lake. Here, we were protected from the trees, and it was so calm, the edge of the lake was mirrored on the surface of the water. A sparrow darted out from the woods on our right, followed closely by a red-tailed hawk. They swooped low over us, and then quickly turned right to fly into the woods again.

Packrat shook his head. "Poor little guy."

"I think he got away." I pointed to a tree stump just ahead of us. The hawk sat there, looking around as if it'd been there all the time. "Being little works in your favor when you're flying through the trees."

Having my friends to talk and laugh with made it seem like no time at all before we arrived at the trailhead. We got out in ankle-deep water to pull the kayaks up onshore, then pulled them the rest of the way into the bushes. Throwing our life jackets inside them with the paddles, we sat down on the rocks to put on our socks and sneakers. Minutes later we were walking one behind the other on the trail. Roy was so excited to finally be here, he took the lead and Packrat and I had all we could do to keep up with him.

"So how do you find an old outhouse hole?" Roy asked, switching his backpack from his left shoulder to his right. One, two, three more steps on the wildlife trail, and then he stopped so suddenly, my face hit the back of his head.

"Ow!" I grabbed my nose, stumbling back into Packrat and stepping on his foot.

"Ow!" Packrat hollered, hopping up and down.

"What the heck?" I cried, wondering if my friend had found signs of a bear or something.

Roy stood on the trail, a hand on each hip. Pointing a finger at each of us in turn, he said, "If you tell anyone, either of ya, that I helped dig up an outhouse hole . . ." Roy let the words hang in the air.

I laughed. "You know, it's not, like, a hole that's still filled with, you know . . ." I turned to Packrat for help.

"Black water," Packrat said simply. Which was what campers called the poop-and-pee combination that came out of the toilet tank on a trailer.

"Right." I wished I'd thought of that perfect explanation. "It's a hundred years old now. It's all turned to dirt."

"So it doesn't smell?" Roy pulled a swimmer's nose clip from his jean pocket. "I won't need this?"

Packrat snorted. "No! It'll be like an archaeological dig."

"Doesn't matter what you call it," said Roy. "Somebody peed and pooped in that hole. A lot of somebodies."

Packrat and I shared a smile. Of the three of us, I wouldn't have guessed Roy to be the squeamish one. We started walking again, single file, along the Old Cellar Hole Trail, Packrat's name for the wildlife trail. Pine, maple, and birch trees were all around us, as far as we could see. I could hear chickadees, woodpeckers, and ravens, though there were way more birds than that out here. Every now and then, I heard the

faint roar of a car or truck, reminding me of what Dad had said about
the road being not too far away.

"So what's the first step?" Packrat asked from behind me. Thanks to
the trip to town, and the thunderstorm warnings that had kept us off the
lake until after lunch, I knew we wouldn't have much time today. How
were we going to find the old privy hole? From what I'd read on the web-
sites of some famous privy hole diggers, it wouldn't be easy. The wooden
outhouse was long gone. And the privy hole itself? It would have been
filled in, and then many years' worth of leaves and dirt would have covered it over until it looked like the rest of the forest floor.

"Well, that one blogger, he said to look for low dips in the land." I
stepped over the fallen tree and pointed off to the left, into the woods.
"Shallow spots. Because it would have settled down over time. We're
supposed to poke around in them to see if the dirt is clay-like. And if we
can find a stone, wood, or brick square under the top layer, where the
outhouse would have sat, it's probably the privy hole."

Roy pushed a maple-tree branch to one side, holding it until I could
grab and hold it for Packrat. "Mr. Goodwin said it was brick-lined."

"He also said his grandfather's story was a legend," Packrat
warned. "I'm not sure I believe the whole throwing-gold-in-the-toilet
part. I mean, digging it up back then would have been gross!"

I laughed. "But throughout history, people have done some weird
stuff to hide their money. And they did dig out the privy holes and cart
off the waste rather than dig a new one. Kind of like our customers
have their motorhomes and trailers pumped out instead of driving them
to the transfer station."

Seeing the beginning of the stone wall, I knew the cellar hole was
to the left. I stepped off the trail to lead the way. "It'd be cool to find
a rare bottle or an old toy or something. You saw how crazy everyone
was over that old blue bottle."

"So why not just dig up more bottles at the cellar hole?" Packrat asked.

I'd thought about that. "I guess because it only has bottles. And we can get back to that anytime. A privy, though, if we can find it, could have all kinds of things. One guy found false teeth!"

"Cooool!" Roy and Packrat said together.

When the Wayside Inn cellar hole and fireplace came into view, Roy whistled low. "You're right. This is a cool spot!" He walked right into the cellar and ran a hand along one of the walls. "Imagine stacking these big stones way back then."

We walked up to the highest spot in the area, which was actually not so high. We turned this way and that, looking for signs of a low spot.

Seeing an area that seemed to fit the description, I said, "Found it!" and started walking toward it. "Ready, guys?"

"Ready," Packrat and Roy said in unison.

Only we weren't all walking in the same direction.

"Where are you going?" I asked.

Packrat pointed left and Roy and I tried to follow the imaginary line from his finger. "There's a great spot over there, next to the stone wall." I could see the low spot he was talking about, but I wasn't convinced.

"Nah." Roy pointed to a different area twenty steps from the cellar wall. "I'm betting on that one over there."

I shook my head. "Too close." I showed them my spot, off to the right, farther away than Packrat's, but still near the wall. Mine was more square and a little bigger, the size I imagined a three-hole privy would be.

"Mine is logical," Roy argued. "Customers wouldn't want to walk far in the middle of the night, when they aren't familiar with where they're going. We should try mine first."

Packrat shook his head. "They wouldn't want the smell right out-side the windows. Mine is away, but close."

"Away is good," I agreed. "But still too close to the inn. They wouldn't want the customers to get a whiff of it when they came out of the building."

We stood in a circle now, staring each other down, each of us thinking we had located the right spot. I wondered how we were going to check all three of them before dark.

"I bet you two," Roy began, in total seriousness, "that my spot is the spot."

Knowing what he was getting at, I grinned. "Every guy on his own?"

"The one who finds the cellar hole wins," Packrat said. He put out his hand, Roy covered it with one of his, and then mine went on top. Betting was something we knew all about.

"The losers have to tell everyone in the campground what an amazing privy hole finder the winner is," I announced.

Packrat's laugh echoed through the woods.

Roy's smile faded. "Wait. I'm not sure if I want to win or lose now."

The three of us got to work.

Chapter 13

One of the most common myths about black bears is that if you get between a mother and her cubs, she is sure to attack. This isn't completely true. She will most likely run at you and stop short to scare you; an attack is rare, but possible.

We'd been searching for the privy hole for less than an hour when Roy called out, "Guys?" I wasn't sure I heard him at first, because it was hesitant. Kind of like a not-sure-if-I-need-you-or-not call. I took my garden hand trowel and stuck it in another spot in the forest floor, digging just six inches or so deep. I hoped to hit gray, clay-like sand that would mean this was a filled-in privy hole. Seeing brown dirt again, I sighed and stood. I'd taken my low spot and made test holes every few feet in rows. It looked like a Connect Four board without the yellow and red checkers.

A minute later I heard Roy call again, this time for sure. "Hey! Guys! I think I actually found that toilet!"

"Privy!" Packrat and I called back. We half-jogged, half-walked through the brush and over logs to get to where Roy stood, looking kind of smug. His shallow area looked like mine, with little holes dug all over the place. One of the holes was deeper than the others.

"Check this out!" Roy crouched down to gently dig up the spot a little more. When I looked inside, I could see shiny green.

"A bottle?" I said.

"Yep, and four bricks in a row over there." He took us to where he'd found them.

Packrat got down on his knees to gently dig along the red brick with his little trowel. "I'll follow these, so we know how big a privy hole we have."

"I'll keep digging up the bottle," Roy said.

"If the privy was really brick-lined, then those bricks would go down kinda far, like a wall," I said, kneeling next to Packrat. "You keep going along to find the frame. I'll dig down to make sure this isn't just an edge for a garden or sidewalk or something."

Packrat nodded and we got to work. I carefully dug the dirt out from both sides of a two-foot length of brick in the dirt. Then I started digging down on the inside. Under the first bricks was a second layer. They were crumbly from being underground so long, so it was slow going. Under those, I found a third layer. This was it; this was the spot! Digging a little wider on the inside, I then went back to digging down. A fourth row! And a fifth!

Noticing that the air had cooled a bit, I stood and put my hand on a large spruce tree to look up at the sun. It was lower than the treetops, halfway to the horizon. Taking my hand off the tree, I went to reach for my water bottle, but I stopped.

I turned back to where my hand had just been.

Scratches. Five long marks, etched deep in the bark. I counted three sets of them on that tree. Two of them looked fresh. On the other side, whole strips of bark had been clawed away.

I reached out a hand to trace the scratch marks. Seeing some long, black hairs snagged in the bark, I pulled them free. Uh-oh. This was a marking tree, a way for bears to communicate with other bears.

"Umm, guys?"

The words weren't even out of my mouth when I heard soft snuffling noises. From the corner of my eye, I saw something black moving through the trees, way behind the cellar hole.

"*Shhhh!*" I warned. Packrat and Roy froze as I pointed in the direction I'd seen the animal.

Packrat dropped flat to the ground. "Get down!" he ordered. "I think I saw . . . No way!"

"Yes, way," I whispered back.

"Do we go up a tree?" Roy slowly moved backward toward us.

Thinking of the scratches I'd just seen, I shook my head. "Uh-uh. In the cellar hole. Behind the wall so it doesn't see us."

"But what if it smells us?" Packrat asked. We stayed crouched low as we very carefully made our way into the cellar and over to where the cellar door would have been.

I lifted my face to the breeze. "We're downwind; I think we should be okay."

One after the other, the three of us peeked around the edge of the wall. Just then, out from under the trees came a big, black bear. We could clearly see a small, white, V-shaped patch on its upper chest. Slowly, the bear stood up on its hind legs and sniffed the air.

And we, just as slowly, slunk down behind the wall.

Chapter 14

Bears see in color and have good vision close up. Their distance vision is not as good.

"That bear's gotta be six feet tall!" Packrat whispered. The three of us were still crouched behind the old cellar hole wall.

"Did you see that notch in its left ear?" Roy whistled low. "I bet it means it's a fighter."

"It's a 'he,' " I told my friends. "Look at his size! He's too huge to be a female!"

One by one, we looked through the cellar door opening again. The bear was still there, standing up, sniffing the air.

"What do we do?" Packrat whispered. We watched as the bear dropped to all fours to continue plodding through the woods with its rolling walk.

As one, we stood there quietly until we could put our hands on the top of the old cellar wall and peek over. The bear was still slowly heading in our general direction.

Cool! thought the nature-geek side of me.

Run for the kayaks! cried my sensible side.

Packrat pulled a small camera from an outside pocket. My nature-geek side won.

The bear didn't seem to be in much of a hurry, really. Every couple of steps, he'd stop to paw the ground, or smell something like a rock or a tree.

"We're good here?" Packrat asked, while taking video of the bear sniffing some bushes.

The more I watched, the more he seemed to be walking at an angle that took him away from us. "Black bears are always looking for food, like berries and plants and acorns and stuff like that. They don't eat other animals very often."

The bear stopped. He pawed the ground again, and sniffed the air. Plodding over to a rotted, leaning tree trunk, he sniffed the base of that, too. Then he sniffed a little higher. The trunk had no branches left on it, and only a little bark here and there. I couldn't even tell what kind of tree it was.

The bear stood up on his hind legs and leaned back on that trunk. I swear he closed his eyes and started wiggling all over the place, up and down, left and right, scratching his back. The trunk wobbled from the weight. Roy laugh-snorted, and when he did, his hand slipped off the top of the wall, pulling a grapefruit-size rock free. It tumbled down the wall, sending a sharp, cracking sound into the woods, once, twice, three times. And then a loud thump, as it hit the ground.

For a second, no one moved. Not us. Not the bear up against the tree trunk. Not even the blue jays that'd been hollering a few seconds ago. The silence was broken when the bear dropped to all four paws to run into the woods.

"Sorry, guys," Roy said, kicking the wall. "Darn it."

I laughed. "Probably for the best."

Packrat moved between us. "Check this out." He held out the camera so we could all see the video of the bear as he foraged, and then scratched his back.

"That's pretty good," I said. Packrat paused the video to zoom in on the back paws of the bear.

"What the heck is that?" Roy asked, taking the camera. Then he passed it to me.

Trailing from the bear's left hind paw was a long strip of white paper, fluttering up like a flag when it walked. "Toilet paper?" I raised an eyebrow.

Roy snorted. Packrat said, "Wonder if his friends will tell him, or let him walk around like that for a while."

"I ain't telling him!" I looked at the picture one more time. It seemed so weird. Toilet paper way out here?

"So, it's safe to stay and finish edging the toilet hole?" Roy asked.

"Privy hole!" Packrat and I corrected. Roy smirked.

I looked at my watch. "We've got an hour. Let's see how much we can do." Looking around the woods, I added, "But someone's on bear-watch duty."

That day, we'd found all four sides. The bricks formed a rectangle, which we guessed was the three-hole privy, like in Mr. Goodwin's town legend. The bottle Roy found turned out to be broken, but it was still cool. It was a sign we'd found the right spot.

Paddling home, Packrat had pulled out a small notebook to write down a list of tools we'd need when we came back. "Imagine," he'd said dreamily, "if we find just a couple gold coins, we'll be famous!"

It was six days later now, and I was still thinking about those coins. I thought about them as Roy, Packrat, and I raked campsites. I thought about them when we camped out overnight and researched. I thought about them this morning when we played Rock, Paper, Scissors to decide which one of us was going to clean bathrooms and who was going to help Dad. And I was thinking about them now, as Roy and I worked side by side with Dad to build the recycling center.

Privy digging.

Gold.

Hidden.

What would Packrat and Roy think about what I wanted to do with my share?

"Cooper!" Dad's voice brought me back to our building project, for the third time in two hours.

Roy frowned at me. "You gotta pay attention. Your dad almost hit you in the head with a two-by-four."

Dad held a nail on the board, aimed the hammer, and pounded it in with one hit. "Roy's right. Where's your mind today, anyway?"

I could take Dad correcting me during a project, but my friend? "I was thinking."

Dad continued to drive in nails. Roy held the other end of the board, and said sharply, "Well, get your head in the game!"

I slowly turned to look at him down the length of the almost-done recycling center. I could tell Roy was all business; no teasing going on here.

Since when did my friend give me work lectures?

Molly skipped around the corner, cutting off my view of Roy. "It looks like a looooong wishing well, Daddy!" She'd been hanging around, bringing Dad nails and whatever tools he needed. And, as usual, talking up a storm when he didn't need anything at all.

The plan for the *recycling* center was to put a bunch of large trash cans with attached, locking lids inside the box. People would put their recycling inside them. Right now, Dad was building a roof, to help keep the rain off the cans.

"We should paint a sign," I said, "and list all the recyclables they can drop off here. We get customers from all over the United States, and different towns and states have different rules."

"Great idea!" Dad clapped a hand on my shoulder. "You sure have a lot of them lately. Can I put you on that job?"

"Sure!"

"Just make sure you spell *recycling* right," Roy said. Did his voice have a bit of an edge to it? I guess not, 'cause Dad didn't seem to hear it. In fact, he chuckled.

"Good advice, Roy. Wish I had a nickel for every sign I painted with a misspelled word. Remember that time I painted 'Barking Lot,' instead of 'Parking Lot'?"

Packrat walked up, stuffing the last bite of a hot dog into his mouth. He raised an eyebrow as he chewed. "Hugh tys till erking on wish?" Which I knew meant, "You guys still working on this?"

"How were the ladies' rooms?" I shot back. We both knew building the recycling shed was way better than cleaning bathrooms. At least, it should have been. But with Roy acting all bossy and stuff, I think I would have rather cleaned the ladies' rooms. Alone.

Dad stood up to put the hammer and bucket of nails in the back of the golf cart. Turning, he checked his handiwork. "Not bad, boys. Not bad at all. It just needs a coat of paint, but that hot dog is making my stomach rumble. Molly, pick up all the little pieces of wood and throw them in the campfire ring, okay?"

" 'Kay!"

"We'll burn them at tonight's fire. Boys, let's gather up these tools—"

A car slowly rolled through the gate and stopped next to us.

"Ms. Marco!" Why was my teacher here again?

Dad leaned down to open her door for her. "Hi! What can we do for you?"

Ms. Marco got out and shut the door. She leaned up against it and sighed heavily. "I'm here to apologize for the mess. Poor Cooper. All you did was write a paper on why it's important to recycle," she said, shaking her head.

Dad picked up a rag from the back of the golf cart and wiped his hands. "We heard from Mr. Goodwin that some of the businesses are trying to fight it."

Ms. Marco looked at me sadly. "What I didn't know was that Mainely Trash would raise their rates just forty-eight hours before the announcement was made."

I gasped. "So they knew? They did it on purpose?"

"Talbot must have told his cousin, Stu," Dad agreed.

"But, that isn't fair!" Roy said.

"It sure isn't," said Ms. Marco. "That's why they're fighting it." She folded her arms. "I'm so upset with all of this. How are you dealing with your trash?"

Dad smiled. "Believe it or not, we're going to be okay." He pointed at the project we'd just finished. "This is a voluntary recycling station. Totally Cooper's idea. We've also hired one of our campers, Lynn, to haul our trash away. She had a good plan, needed the paycheck. And having her do it means I can be here to get my daily jobs done."

Ms. Marco's face brightened. "Does she want more work? There are people who'd love to get their trash hauled."

"I can ask," Dad said. "But listen, I've already given Mr. Goodwin her name. I don't want to overload her."

"Can't hurt to ask!" Ms. Marco said.

"Can't hurt at all!" Dad agreed.

Chapter 15

Black bears can live thirty years or more in the wild.

After we'd finished picking up, Roy, Packrat, and I gathered up tools for our dig, and booked it to our kayaks. Halfway to the privy site, we saw a dark-haired woman in a yellow shirt wave to us from her kayak.

"Do we know her?" Roy squinted and put a hand up to block the sun, to try to see better.

I took another look and laughed. "It's Warden Kate!" Without her usual green uniform and baseball cap, we'd almost paddled right past her.

"I have today off," she called, as we paddled up alongside. "Looks like you found some time to get out on the lake today, too. An afternoon of fishing?"

Taking turns with the story, Packrat, Roy, and I quickly filled her in on our plans to dig up the old privy. "Interesting," she said. "I've met a lot of people who think a good bottle dump is like finding buried treasure. But I've never heard of privy digging."

"You find all kinds of things excavating a privy," I said. "Buttons, toys, jugs, and more. Not just bottles."

"And it's more fun to say," Roy smirked. "Privy digging."

"Just be careful," she warned, but she wore a smile. "You boys are a trouble magnet. And speaking of trouble . . ." Warden Kate's face got serious. "I almost forgot to ask: What did your parents decide to do about hauling the campground trash away, Cooper? Are you using Mainely Trash?"

"No, Dad hired a camper and her son to haul it to the incinerator," I said.

"Really? I'm glad he found another trash hauler. I'll spread the word. Maybe we can get some of the protesters to change their minds and use your camper, too."

"Protesters?" Packrat wondered. "Like, with signs and stuff?"

"No." Warden Kate's brows furrowed with worry. "Since the transfer station closed on Monday, the hardware store and the florist have been letting their trash pile up. Kind of like a boycotting thing. They hope the town manager will change his mind and let businesses use the new transfer station if he sees how horrible it looks when he travels around town." She shook her head. "Talbot is so stubborn, he'll never change his mind."

A warm breeze started to blow my kayak backwards, and I put out a hand to grab her kayak to stay close.

"There are also some homeowners who are pretty mad the transfer station is closed, so they're letting their trash pile up, too," she added. "It's already beginning to stink and attract animals."

"Really? Like what kind?" Roy paddled forward, then backward, then forward again, trying to stay near us.

"Ravens, raccoons, possums, and foxes have been reported." She sighed heavily. "And, of course, bears."

"Bears!" All three of us said it at the same time.

"Whoa," I added. "Maybe that explains the toilet paper hanging off the paw of that bear we saw."

Warden Kate's lips twitched with a smile. "What? Where?"

"At the cellar hole. It came walking by—" When the warden raised an eyebrow and gave me a what-were-you-thinking look, I added, "We watched from far away."

A loon gave a low, sad wail from the other end of the lake. The one nearer to us answered. Warden Kate looked their way, but I could tell she was thinking about what I'd said.

"That's kind of far to have traveled from town and not have it fall off," she said. "But I suppose anything is possible. How big was the bear?"

I looked to Packrat for help. "I don't know, maybe five, six feet?"

Warden Kate opened her mouth, but a radio crackled before she could say anything. I put my hand to my waist at the same time as Warden Kate did. But it wasn't my camp radio.

"Two bears sighted on Dogwood Lane. Not responding to loud noises. Need additional backup."

Warden Kate sighed. "I was afraid of this. When one comes after trash, there's always more behind. And with the record number of bears this year . . . Well, so much for my day off. This trash problem is becoming a real mess." She picked up her paddle, laughing at her own joke. "I'll see you later, boys." Pointing the end of her paddle at us, she put on her serious game warden expression. "Be careful."

"We will." I gave her kayak a gentle shove, to push her off. "You be careful, too," I called, thinking of the bear.

We paddled quickly, and it didn't take long before we reached the shore, had the kayaks tucked away in the bushes, and stepped onto the Old Cellar Hole Trail. We hadn't even taken three steps when Packrat stilled. "Did you hear that?"

Immediately thinking of the bear track we'd seen last time, I looked around on the ground. "I don't hear—"

"Shhhh!" Roy raised his hand. He turned his head slightly toward the water. "A bird call?"

"Yeah." We all turned back toward the lake. A minute later, I heard it too. A faint, seagull kind of cry. But it was all wrong, like it was finding it hard to make the noise. I searched up and down the pebbled shoreline, listening.

"This way," I whispered, pointing left.

It didn't take long to find the ring-billed gull. We crouched behind a downed tree trunk to watch it. The poor thing was walking weird, taking three steps to the left and one to the right. Staggering. It didn't even notice us. Was it hurt?

We half-crawled, half-crouched our way over the tree trunk. Packrat pulled out his binoculars, put them to his eyes, and gasped. He handed them to me as he explained to Roy, "It's hard to see from here, but it has string or line or something tangled around his neck."

"And around a leg!" I said, zooming in with the binoculars.

Packrat took off his vest. He put his hand in one of the large, inside back pockets and pulled out a piece of netting.

We knew what we had to do.

Moving ever so slowly along the shoreline, we tried not to frighten the white and gray gull. If it struggled, it might tighten the line around itself even more. When we found a high spot, with the shoreline below us, I whispered, "This is perfect. I'll wait here with the net. You two go into the woods, and come back around toward me on the shore. Make lots of noise so the gull moves my way. And when it's below me—"

"You'll drop the net!" Roy nodded.

"Got it," Packrat added.

My friends went into the woods behind me. I didn't hear them for a couple of minutes, and I began to wonder if maybe they'd gone the wrong way. But I shouldn't have worried. They can be quiet when they need to, and loud when they want to. Sticks cracked under their feet. Rocks skidded down the shoreline. I winced to see the gull scurry as fast as it could in a limp-drag-waddle in my direction. But there was no other way to catch it.

I crouched beside a boulder and hoped it would be so worried about Packrat and Roy that it wouldn't notice me.

"One," I whispered to myself, as the gull came closer and closer still. "Two. Three!" I stood to drop the netting. It landed right on the seagull, which immediately started hopping around on its yellow legs.

I scrambled down to meet my friends. Roy reached into his back pocket to pull out his utility knife, while Packrat bundled up the netting until he had the seagull firmly, but gently, in his arms. Roy handed me the little scissors and I rolled back a corner of the netting to check the line.

But this wasn't fishing line.

Packrat raised an eyebrow, as all three of us exchanged what-the-heck looks. What were the odds that the gull would find and then get tangled in dental floss? I mean, out here? Lakeside?

The floss was wrapped around the lower part of the gull's yellow beak, just above the black ring that gives it its name. From there, it wound around its left leg and back through the beak. The poor thing could only open its beak a quarter-inch or so. When it moved its leg, the floss pulled back to cut into the skin at the joint between the upper and lower halves. If we hadn't found this little guy, the floss would have kept cutting deep into its skin. It wouldn't have survived long, not being able to eat or fly.

Very, very carefully, Packrat tucked one side of the seagull's head against his shoulder, and shielded its yellow eyes with his hand. I slowly reached over with the scissors. *Snip. Snip.* With each quick sound, the seagull gave a tiny jump. Its webbed feet pushed against Packrat's stomach.

"One more should do it," I whispered. "Be ready to open the net so he doesn't peck you."

Snip.

Packrat opened his arms, lifting the gull up as if offering him back to the sky. The ring-billed gull unfurled its wings, and in an instant, was airborne. Flying down the lake, the bird called for all the world to hear, "I'm free! I'm free!"

Well, that was our translation.

Fifteen minutes later, we made it—finally—to the old Wayside Inn privy site. Packrat set down the basket of tools. He pulled three gardening trowels out of his inside vest pockets, then looked at me expectantly.

I dropped the shovels I'd lugged from our kayaks, while Roy spread out the tarp that would collect the dirt we dug and any artifacts we found. "Time to dig," I said.

Starting with shovels, we carefully dug out the first couple feet of dirt. We didn't just throw it out of the way, though. Instead, we put it on the tarp, so we could fill in the hole when we were done. Everything we'd read said we probably wouldn't find any artifacts this early, but we couldn't help but look. Other than the broken bottle Roy had found yesterday, we didn't see anything interesting.

Another half a foot down, and the dirt changed to a dark, dark brown. Almost black.

"We hit a trash layer!" I threw my shovel out of the hole, beyond the tarp. "This is where the newspaper article said we'd start to find stuff. So only small digs now," I reminded them. Their shovels joined mine, and we all took hold of a trowel.

Crouching down, I began scraping the dirt carefully, looking for anything that didn't belong. Once I had a little pile of dirt, I scooped it into a bucket. When the bucket was full, I stood to dump it on the tarp and push it around, looking for any small stuff. Each of us took a third of the hole to work. I had the right, Roy had the left, and Packrat was in the middle. And let me tell you, there wasn't much wiggle room.

Sweat beaded at the back of my neck and slowly, slowly slid down until it slipped under my shirt collar. I shuddered at the tickling sensation, and resisted the urge to rub the spot, because my hands were covered with black dirt.

Crouching in one position for so long made my back and legs hurt, so I stood up to stretch out the aches. Putting one arm behind my back, I leaned back from the waist as far as I could, lifting my other arm over my head.

Suddenly, I was falling over Packrat, who had bent over to dig at the very bottom of the hole. He fell into Roy, who fell face-first into the brick wall.

"Hey! You okay?" I asked, leaning over Packrat to check on him.

Roy turned, sputtering and spitting. *"Blech! Ptooey!"* Doubled over now, his spit landed by my sneakers. "I think I ate some!"

"Ewww! Ate some *what?*" I cried. "A bug? A worm?" *A spider?* Even I shuddered at that last thought.

"Worse! One-hundred-and-fifty-year-old poop!"

Packrat and I exchanged what-the-heck-is-he-talking-about looks. But then, the two of us realized exactly what Roy was saying. He'd eaten privy dirt. Packrat slapped a hand over his own mouth, eyes twinkling. I coughed. Then I snickered. I tried to hide my face. But the laugh inside me was like a balloon being filled with air, and I couldn't help it. I just burst out laughing.

Just like that, cool black dirt was raining down on me, sliding under my shirt collar, falling at my feet. And when it stopped, there stood Roy, his dirt bucket high over my head. For a second, I wanted to shove him. But then I realized two things: One, Roy had a smile, which meant this wasn't an angry-getting-back at me move, more like an oh-yeah-see-how-you-like-it prank; and two, I deserved it.

We all decided, then and there, that the hole wasn't big enough for the three of us. So Packrat went up top first, while Roy and I scraped and gently dug from wall to wall. When it was time to empty our buckets, Packrat reached down to lift them out, and gave them back empty.

An hour later, with a little over three feet dug, I was up top, and Packrat and Roy were digging. I looked down at the tarp and realized it'd been a while since we'd found anything. So far, we only had the broken green bottle Roy had found, two rusty and bent nails, and a small piece of rough brown glass. The sun no longer shone brightly overhead, and the breeze had cooled a bit. I looked at my watch. Five o'clock? Probably time—

"Found something!" Packrat's voice came from deep in the hole. He was kneeling, digging into the floor. I bent over the edge above, while Roy stood behind Packrat's shoulder.

"I think it's a bowl. A big one." He didn't look up. With a gloved hand, he pushed the dirt away from the find. A white ceramic piece the size of a dollar bill poked up through the dirt. After a minute or two, he pulled his gloves off to be able to dig under it with his fingers. More and more of the shape began to show through, and it was twice the size of any bottle we'd found so far.

"Whoa!" Packrat cried. "It's a pitcher." Using his pointer and middle fingers, he dug down and under one side to gently pry it from the dirt. When it popped out and he lifted it up, we all groaned in frustration. It was only half a pitcher. The half with the handle. The other half lay in pieces in the dirt.

"Darn it," Roy said.

"I thought we had something this time," I agreed.

Packrat nodded. "It does look old, though." Handing up the half to me, he grinned. "We're just getting started!"

I held out my hand to Packrat, and helped him climb out. Then I held out my hand to Roy, and a loud rumbling sound filled the air.

"Sorry," Roy said, taking my hand. "I'm hungry."

It was getting late. Close to suppertime. "We should head back," I said, although I really, really wanted to stay and dig a little more, since we'd finally found something. I couldn't help but wonder what else was in there. More bottles? Pots?

Dare I hope, gold?

Chapter 16

Large forests are the perfect habitat for black bears.
Nuts and berries provide food, and females with cubs
like to climb the large trees when they sense danger.

Packrat had moaned about having to get up before the sun. He had groaned putting on his life jacket and climbing in the kayak. He had grumbled about the heavy, gray, swirling fog we were paddling through.

After half a mug of hot cocoa, though, he'd started paddling a little faster. I knew he was remembering the ceramic pitcher we'd found yesterday. It'd told us two things: One, people in the old days did use that privy as a trash can, not just a toilet; and two, we might find something even cooler.

Now we were back to digging at the three-foot-deep mark, very, very carefully. We didn't want to accidentally break something or go so fast that we shoveled out the little stuff without seeing it. There wasn't a lot of room in the privy hole, so we each had a job to do. I carefully scooped dirt into a box screen we'd made from a square, wooden frame with wire mesh on the bottom. Roy shook the frame, and the dirt fell through the mesh holes, leaving behind small items. So far, the only stuff left in the screen was rocks. Rocks in every color, size, and shape.

The dirt that fell through went into a bucket. Once we'd filled the bucket, Packrat pulled it up and out of the hole by a rope, and dumped it on a pile two feet away. Every twenty minutes or so, we switched jobs, 'cause we all wanted the cool job of sifting the dirt, hoping to be the first to find an old coin.

Or a ring.

Or a piece of gold.

Soon we had dug another foot down. So far, all we'd found were broken pieces of ceramic pots. But even those, we were saving on a tarp off to the side of the dig.

"Ready for me to pull up the bucket?" Packrat asked from up above. He took hold of the rope that was tied to the bucket at my feet.

"Wait!" Roy cried. He shook the screen again. *Clink, clink.* And again. *Clink.* I dropped my trowel to crouch beside the screen. Every time he shook it, we heard *Clink. Clink. Clink.* A metal-against-metal sound.

I got goose bumps on my arms. Could it be?

With every shake, more and more of a round, dull, metal object appeared through the dirt. I reached out to pick it up out of the screen. "A button!" I rubbed it on my jeans before holding it out in my palm. Packrat jumped down in the hole with us. Reaching into a pocket, he pulled out a magnifying glass.

It looked like it might be brass, but it was so tarnished and dirty from lying in the dirt for maybe a hundred years, that we had a hard time knowing for sure. The flat metal button was just smaller than an inch wide, and had a raised, five-pointed star in the middle. A bunch of tiny raised stars ran around the outside edge. I scraped at them with my fingernail. One, two, three, four . . . seventeen in all! I flipped it over to find a small metal loop sticking out, probably for sewing onto a shirt or coat. Words were etched around the loop in a circle, but I could only make out a capital S, T, and D. My whole body wanted to jump up and down. I felt like I had springs in my legs. Packrat and I grinned at each other. Finally! Something interesting!

Roy took out his phone "Darn it! No service. I forgot. We'll have to figure out what we've got here when we get home."

Whoa! Our first big find. It wasn't gold, but it sure was cool! I didn't know about my friends, but now I wanted to dig deeper, faster! But I knew faster was a bad idea. We might miss something, or worse, break it in our hurry.

We dug for another hour or so as the sun climbed higher and higher. We were about five feet down now, and the brick privy walls went up over our heads. The dirt at this level was a dark, rich color.

We ate a quick lunch and then it was time to switch jobs again. I grabbed hold of the rope, which was now tied to a nearby tree, and put one foot on the brick wall. As I crawled over the top, I noticed how much warmer it was out here, compared to down in the hole.

Packrat climbed down the rope for his turn with the screen. Roy moved to do some digging. With his first scrape of the trowel, we all heard a *thunk*.

"Whoops!" Roy said, wincing. Putting the trowel down, he began to dig with his hands. I held my breath, and Packrat leaned over his shoulder.

"Just a root," Roy said, studying it. "A big one. Gonna need root cutters." He ran the back of his hand over his forehead, leaving a brown streak there. I grinned.

"Sure you want to be wiping your face with privy dirt?" I asked, trying to keep my voice innocent-sounding.

Roy's eyes widened. He pulled his T-shirt up and began scrubbing his face. Packrat laughed out loud. Teasing him about the privy dirt hadn't gotten old yet.

I pulled up the bucket and carried it to the dirt pile on the tarp. Then I lowered it back into the hole, empty. "Could you cut the root with a big shovel?" I asked.

Roy shook his head. "It's a good two inches around. Did we bring any cutters?"

Packrat called up to me, "I have a pair in my vest, but they're more for smaller stuff. Better add cutters to the list of things we have to bring next time."

"We probably should dig around it first anyway," I said.

Roy nodded, "For a little bit—"

A noise caught my attention. I tipped my head to one side and looked off into the woods.

"What?" Roy asked.

Packrat climbed out to stand beside me. "If that bear comes back, I don't want to be stuck in a hole."

"Do you hear it?" I asked, as Roy climbed out too.

We stood silently, listening. There it was again! Clinking sounds, like two bottles hitting each other.

The clinking went away. Now, I heard crunching leaves, and a small, stifled cry. The three of us slowly walked toward the sounds, and found ourselves staring at a heavy thicket of young pine trees. Packrat pointed, and I saw several of the saplings move as if a breeze had caught them.

Only there was no breeze.

Roy pointed first to himself, then to the left, and moved off in that direction. Packrat did the same, to the right. I stayed in the middle. When we had the area surrounded, my friends drove whatever it was my way. *Clap. CLAP. CLAP!*

In a burst, a reddish ball half-bounded, half-rolled out toward me. Not a ball.

A fox kit!

And the poor thing had its head in a jar!

Packrat and Roy came up behind it, shaking their heads sadly.

"It must have gotten caught just a little while ago," I said.

"It's not dehydrated, right?" Roy asked. "Its nose looks wet."

Packrat drew two pairs of gloves from his pockets, throwing one pair to Roy and the other to me. Roy and I surrounded the kit, who was obviously exhausted from trying to break free. It was panting and shaking.

"I wonder how long it's been caught up like this?" I muttered. Packrat took off his vest and gently threw it over the kit. I scooped up the bundle, tucking it in my elbow like you would hold a cat in one arm.

We'd learned how to do this from Warden Kate, when fox kits on my property had been kit-napped.

With my gloved hands, I tucked the vest in under the fox to keep his paws bundled up and safe. Then I pulled back the part of the coat that was over the bottle, and the kit's face. "Poor little kit," I crooned softly. "We've got you now."

The little kit's eyes rolled from Packrat to me and back again. I wondered how well it could see through the jar. It squirmed in my arm, and I held it more tightly. But not too tightly.

Roy glanced up at me with a worried frown. "Just pull it off?"

"Try it," I said.

Roy took hold of the clear glass jar and tugged gently. He twisted it just a bit, but it looked like it wasn't going to come off easily. Roy looked above and below the bottle. The kit had gone limp in my arms, almost as if it knew we were trying to help.

Packrat took a look, too. He moved the jar a little to the left. Then the right. "I think I see how to do it." His eyes turned to me.

"Go for it," I said, holding the kit a tiny bit tighter.

Taking hold of the jar with one hand, he held the kit by the scruff of its neck in the other. Twisting the jar just a tiny bit, he tipped it to one side, then downward. The combination popped the jar off the kit's head. The little fox blinked chocolate-brown eyes once, twice. It squirmed, but I didn't want to drop it, so I tightened my hold again. "We just want to check you over," I whispered.

Its head was wet, probably from the inside of the jar. Since it was twisting its neck to look at us all, I didn't think it had broken or sprained anything. An ear twitched, and it shivered. From fear, I knew.

I pulled the vest back up over its head and put the whole bundle on the ground. We backed away, as I called, "You can go, little guy!"

The bundle didn't move.

"Go on—"

Two sharp barks rang out from the woods beyond the kit. The mother! The three of us backed away even more. The bundle wiggled. One little brown nose came out from under. It sniffed. One pointed ear was next, then a second. Finally, the kit's whole head emerged from under Packrat's vest. The kit stilled and looked around.

Its eyes met mine.

The mother fox barked again.

The kit took off running.

"Whoa," Packrat breathed.

"That was kinda cool," Roy added.

It was cool. But what the heck was going on? This was the second time this week we'd found an animal caught up in some kind of trash. If we hadn't been in the right place at the right time, they both would have died.

Something was going on. But what?

Chapter 17

Only the female bear raises the cubs. She'll stay with
her cubs through two winter hibernations.

Packrat, Roy, and I watched the kit take off into the woods. I imagined it reuniting with its mother and telling her, "Did you see that? I got my head stuck in a weird, little, see-through cave! Then these giants came and they pulled me out. But I showed them—I got away!"

"My poor little kit! Were you afraid?"

"Nah. It was cool!"

I searched the area. There was no trash in sight. We didn't hear any other people. The jar that'd been on the kit's head was not an old one, like from the bottle dump. In fact, it still had the label on it: HELLMAN'S MAYONNAISE.

"What the heck?" I wanted to throw it on the ground, and stomp on it. Where had it come from? There were no houses around here. No roads. "I'm searching the area," I said.

"Right behind you," said Roy.

We hiked a wide circle around the dig site. Hearing the faint rumble of a truck traveling on Pine Road, it gave me in idea. "I know it's kinda far, but maybe this jar was on the side of the road?" I suggested.

"Hey, that makes sense," said Packrat, his face brightening. "More sense than what I was thinking."

"What were you thinking?" Roy said.

"That maybe somebody was trying to trap the kits, like this past April."

"That doesn't explain the seagull," I pointed out.

"True," Packrat admitted.

We walked in silence for a bit, looking at the base of trees, between rocks, under brush. Nothing was out of place, no sign of humans.

The only thing we found was fresh bear scat. That bear had been back through.

I looked at my watch. "Darn it. We've used up the last hour with the fox. It's time to go back."

"Really?" Roy picked up a stick and swatted a bush. "Mommy gonna be worried again?"

Heat rose up my neck and to my ears, but I took a deep breath and tried to stay cool. It'd been a long time since Roy had given me attitude about my parents setting curfews for me. I decided to try to reason with him.

"I promised Mom I'd be home in plenty of time for supper so we could all eat together. It's three o'clock, and by the time we get all the tools, hike to the kayaks—"

He turned away, heading back to the dig site. Packrat and I did all the talking, all the deciding. Like how we were going to leave a few of the bigger tools—like the long-handled shovels, the bucket, tarp, and screen—by the cellar hole, stashed in some bushes. We gathered a bunch of downed branches and, using some nylon rope, we wove a cover for the privy hole, so no one could see it from a distance. We put all of the treasure we'd found so far in a second bucket, and we took that with us. Except the button. That was extra special, so Packrat put it in one of his many pockets and zipped the pocket shut. All in all, it took close to two hours before we were on the water, heading home.

After just a couple of minutes of paddling, the sound of chirping crickets filled the air. Not real crickets, but the ringtone on my phone.

"I forgot, we have no bars at the dig site," I said as I reached for the phone in my shorts' pocket. I didn't get to it in time, so instead, I listened to the message Mom had left.

"Hey, Roy," I called. I still had the phone to my ear, but I knew he'd want to hear this. "Your dad's at the camp!"

Roy's head whipped around to look back at me. It was the first time he'd looked at me since we'd rescued the kit. His eyes were curious, as I listened to more of the message, and repeated it back to him. "He's looking for you."

Roy nodded once, turned back around, and kept paddling slowly. Packrat and I exchanged looks. Our friend was acting weird. We wanted to know why, but we knew better than to ask. Roy had never been a sharer of personal stuff. But just in case he wanted to, this time, we paddled a little faster until our kayaks were on either side of him. No matter what, we were there for him.

The only sound we heard on the trek back, though, was our paddles dipping into the water. The campground beach came into sight, and he still hadn't said a word. In fact, Roy seemed to drag his feet, moving even more slowly, as we put the kayaks away and walked up toward the office.

As we passed Moose Trail Road, I looked and saw my dad's truck stopped in the middle of it, next to a car going the other way. I knew that car.

"Isn't that your dad?" I asked Roy, tugging on his sleeve for him to follow me.

Mr. Parker and my father stood outside of their vehicles, talking. At least, I think they were talking. Their hands were waving a mile a minute, and their faces looked a little like they were mad at each other.

My friends and I walked a little faster. As we got closer, I could tell the men weren't mad-mad, but they weren't agreeing either.

"Dad?" Roy looked to them both, but stood closer to my father. "What's up?"

Mr. Parker wore a business suit, red-and-blue-striped tie, and shiny black dress shoes. He looked out of place in the campground, especially next to my dad, who had on work jeans, boots, and a buttoned-up denim shirt with our campground name on the pocket.

"Nothing, really," Mr. Parker said. "I was passing through. Thought I'd check in."

The two of them looked at each other, without really seeing each other. Mr. Parker seemed like he wanted to say more, and Roy, like he wanted him to say less.

Roy broke the silence first. "You gonna stop in and see Mom?"

Funny thing; it sounded more like a challenge than a question.

Mr. Parker looked at his watch. "I don't have time—"

"Big surprise."

I looked to Packrat, who looked back at me with a raised eyebrow.

"Roy, I don't have time to argue. I came to tell you something. All of you. So you could hear it from me." Mr. Parker exchanged a look with my dad, who nodded in a go-ahead kind of way. "The client that called the other night?" Mr. Parker cleared his throat. "Well, he's right here in town."

"Here?" Roy's voice went sharp. On edge. I moved a little closer, to show support.

His dad cleared his throat. "The client is Mainely Trash."

"WHAT!" Roy shouted. "Dad! How could you? So you know what they've been doing, right?"

My dad watched Roy carefully. Mr. Parker's face was tight, but his eyes were sad. "I don't have a choice, son. They've been a client of mine since way before this whole trash business. Since before they had their first garbage truck, even."

"Are they suing Cooper's family?" Packrat's worried eyes looked from him to my dad.

"No," Mr. Parker said quickly. "Nothing like that. A group of businesses in town are suing them for going up on their rates, quickly and unfairly. So Mainely Trash has me handling the case, defending them—"

"It was unfair," Roy's voice was half-pleading, half-angry. "Why the heck are you taking their side?"

"Son, it's not that simple." Mr. Parker put a hand on Roy's shoulder, but Roy shrugged it off to move closer to my dad. He hesitated, then squared his shoulders. His voice low and determined, he said, "If you take this case, I won't ever talk to you again. I won't visit you."

My head swiveled to see Packrat's reaction to this. *Visit him?* Packrat looked just as confused as I was.

"Don't say that, buddy." Mr. Parker sounded tired and sad.

"I'm not your buddy! *Buddy* means we actually hang out and do stuff, like Cooper and his dad. It means we like each other!" Roy's voice had gotten hard and mean.

"Roy, your father has to do his job," said my dad, stepping in. "It won't affect me or Cooper or our business. We've got it all figured out for the camp—"

"But it could hurt Mr. Goodwin. And I like Mr. Goodwin. In fact, I think I see more of Mr. Goodwin in the summer than I see of you!" Roy stopped. In a quieter voice, he asked, "Did you tell Mom?"

Mr. Parker nodded. "She's not happy, either. And while we don't agree on a lot of things lately, at least she understands that I don't have a choice. It's my client. It's what I do."

Roy crossed his arms. I knew that meant two things: One, he wasn't budging on what he thought about this whole thing; and two, he was madder than a bee that'd been swatted.

Mr. Parker moved toward Roy, but my friend's narrowed eyes stopped him. He looked helplessly at my dad, then sighed. To Roy, he said, "You know how to reach me, if you or your mom need me."

Another car turned down the camp road to slowly roll toward our group. Dad put his hand up and raised one finger to show we'd be a minute. "Your dad's in a tough spot here, Roy. Mr. Goodwin isn't in any trouble or anything—"

"But his store will close and he'll lose his business if he doesn't win this," Roy pointed out.

"He did say that." Dad wasn't one to hold back the truth, even from kids. "But please, don't let your dad go while you're still mad." My dad put his hand on Roy's shoulder, and Roy leaned into him a bit. Mr. Parker seemed a little smaller, somehow. I felt kind of bad for him.

Roy's shoulders slumped. He opened his mouth to say something.

"Excuse me, Jim?" A lady leaned out the window of the car behind us. When no one said anything, she got out to walk over. Whatever Roy had been about to say was gone, because he had that mad look on his face again.

Dad tried to get Roy to stay, but my friend stomped away. Mr. Parker sighed, before turning to open his car door. Putting one leg inside, he hesitated, then looked at us over the door. "Cooper? Packrat? Keep an eye on him for me, would you?"

"You bet," I said. Packrat only nodded, and turned to follow Roy.

"Sorry to interrupt," the lady said, as Mr. Parker slowly drove away. "But my trash can is overflowing. Is anyone coming to empty it today?"

Dad lifted his hat to scratch his head. "She should have gotten to it an hour ago, but I'll check for you."

Lynn and Charlie were behind on trash pickup already? I thought. *So how would they ever be able to keep up?*

Chapter 18

Unlike cats, black bears have non-retractable claws;
their claws are always out.

Mom said supper was going to be held up, due to some campers checking in late. We'd hurried back for nothing! But I knew better than to complain; she couldn't help it. So I asked Packrat for the button and did a little research, then headed over to the game room to share my findings with Packrat and Roy. I'd only been there five minutes, but it was pretty obvious Roy was working out his anger by beating Packrat soundly at Eight Ball for the third time in a row.

As Roy put the fifteen pool balls in the triangular-shaped rack, I silently asked Packrat how Roy was doing. He lifted his hand and wiggled it back and forth in a so-so kinda way

"You break." Roy lifted the rack.

"Go ahead—" Packrat began.

"I won last! Your turn!" Roy threw the white ball across the pool table top, narrowly missing the perfectly set pool balls.

Packrat caught it, and put it on the green felt tabletop. Bending over, he lined up his shot. I could tell from his hunched shoulders he wasn't enjoying the game all that much. Closing one eye, he looked down his pool stick, pulling it back and forth, back and forth, across his index finger. Then he hit the white ball, knocking it into the triangle of balls, sending them rolling in all directions. Not one rolled into any of the six pockets along the side of the table. His turn was over.

Roy didn't say a word, didn't look our way. He was all business as he hit the white ball with his pool stick, sending it into an all-red, solid ball, knocking it into a corner pocket. "I call solids."

It'd been a long time since I'd seen Roy so bottled-up angry. I felt bad for the guy. I mean, I usually got together with him and Packrat at least twice over the winter to ice-fish or snowshoe. And we'd hung out on the weekends since we opened the campground mid-April. But he'd never said a word about his parents fighting or he and his dad not getting along. Worse, Packrat and I suspected there was more, much more. But I didn't know how to ask, because watching him work the table right now, he looked like a snake, all coiled up, ready to strike at any moment.

I couldn't imagine what he was going through. My parents worked a lot of hours, like his dad, but they were always together, took days off together, ate together. They laughed and joked all the time. The only time they'd ever been separated, that I could remember, was when Dad was in the hospital this past April after a tree had fallen on him. Did they fight? Yeah. But they always worked it out. So, I wasn't sure I could find the words to make my friend feel better, if that was even possible.

But maybe I could distract him from whatever was bugging him.

"Hey! Guess what?" I dug deep in my pocket for the button. "I just did a quick online search for the words *old, button,* and *stars.*"

"What'd you find out?" Packrat asked.

"It's a Maine Militia button!" I handed it to him. "The big star, that's the North Star. These were used from the late 1700s to the early 1800s."

Packrat held the button out toward Roy, but he just grunted and took another shot.

"How much do you think it's worth?" Packrat asked, turning the button over in his hand.

"Well, it's not in great condition. Maybe forty dollars—if we're lucky." I hesitated. Roy was not interested in the button anymore. Time to try something else. "I've been thinking, you know. About the treasure." Roy hit the solid two ball into the left corner pocket.

"Me too!" Packrat sent me a nothing-is-working look. "I think I want to buy a new kayak. One of those fancy fishing ones, with a sail and pedals so I can glide through the water without paddling."

Roy shot again, and this time, the white ball hit a solid three ball, which nudged a solid seven. I thought they were both going to fall into the pocket, but only the three ball did. The seven seemed to hover on the edge for a second or two, then it rolled back half an inch and stopped. Roy stared at that ball, and I swear it shivered in fear. When his scowl deepened, Packrat pulled a cube of blue chalk out of one of his pockets and handed it to him. Roy rubbed it on the edge of his pool stick and went back to studying the balls on the table.

"Well, I thought about buying something for me. And I thought about giving it to my dad to help buy that pool liner. But you know," I said, keeping one eye on Roy as I talked, knowing he was lost in his own dark thoughts, "I think I want to give my share to Charlie and his mom."

Roy stood up straight, the scowl back on his face. He dropped the fat end of the pool stick down on the game-room floor once. "What? You want to give a thief your share?"

Whoa. I looked out the open windows, hoping Charlie wasn't around to hear him. "Hey, keep your voice down. He's just a kid who wanted to get his mom a birthday present, but doesn't even have enough money to buy a little wooden loon. Think about that, Roy. If we want a three-dollar souvenir, our parents have enough change in their pockets to buy one. None of us has to worry about that."

Packrat nodded. "True."

"You don't know what you'd do if you were him. He felt guilty, and 'fessed up to my mom. She tried to give the loon to him, but he wouldn't take it."

Roy just went back to the table. As he ran it, sinking solid after solid, Packrat gave me a sad look. We each leaned against a side of the door frame to watch our friend. *Smack.* Roll, drop. *Smack.* Roll, drop. Roy moved around the pool table, eyeing his shots, until all he had left was the eight ball. Sink that, and he'd win the game without Packrat ever getting another shot on the table.

Packrat gave me a hey-I-have-an-idea look, as he stood straight up. "Hey! You guys want to camp out on my site—"

A horrible whiny motor noise filled the air. It was almost dark now, so all I saw were headlights coming in the gate. Whatever the vehicle was, it was big and annoying-sounding.

"—and my mom will make some hot cocoa and we can make s'mores. I have Reese's peanut butter cups. Your favorite!"

Roy grunted while lining up his last, possibly winning, shot.

"Great!" Packrat took Roy's wordless answer as a yes-that'd-be-cool. Digging in an outside pocket, he said, "I gotta make sure I have the marshmallows—"

The whiny, creaky noise got louder still as the big vehicle turned the corner. Roy took his shot.

BANG! The muffler backfired and Roy hit the left edge of the white ball, sending it in the wrong direction.

"What the heck!" he cried. Banging his pool stick on the floor in frustration, he stormed over to join us at the door. The vehicle's brake lights went on, and I thought from the size of it that it was an old motorhome. Once it rolled under the single spotlight at the new recycling station, I got a better look.

It was an old, beat-up garbage truck with the words MAINELY TRASH on the driver-side door.

"Why are they here?" I walked out the front door of the game room, keeping my sights on the driver door that had just opened.

Packrat caught up to me on my left, and Roy, on my right.

The driver climbed down out of the truck and, without even shutting his door, started walking around the station.

"Can I help you?" I meant to make my voice sound customer-servicey, but it came out more like a what-the-heck-are-you-doing question.

"Just looking," he said, like he was in a grocery store, checking out how ripe the bananas were.

"What? Are you the recycling police, or something?" Roy crossed his arms.

Hearing Roy's sarcastic tone, he finally took some interest in us. I noticed that this round little man with the red suspenders had a small grin, like he thought we were just some kids hanging out. And for some reason, that really made me mad.

"This is my campground and my recycling station. What do you want?" I asked.

The man's eyes widened. "Your campground?" Then he laughed. "I see. Where's your father?"

"I'm right here." I hadn't heard Dad coming. He looked the man up and down, as Roy moved to stand next to him like a bodyguard.

"I'm Stu. Stu Talbot." The man held out his hand.

My dad hesitated. His eyebrow went up a bit, then his hand clasped Stu's and they shook.

Stu took out his clipboard and pulled a pen from his pocket. "So where are you putting the dumpster?" He flipped through a few papers, then pointed over his shoulder toward the recycling station. "I don't see that you've gotten the space ready for it. It'll be another hundred dollars and a two-week wait, since we'll have to do it for you—"

"I see you didn't get my message." Dad rocked back on his heels. One side of his mouth started to curl up, then it went down, then it went up again, like Dad was trying to keep down a satisfied grin.

I didn't keep it down, though. I smiled wide.

Stu looked up at Dad, his pen frozen in midair. "Message?"

"I already have a trash service," Dad said firmly. "They started today."

"You—" Stu tipped his head to one side. "Have? They did?"

Dad kept right on going. "Yes. I'm sorry, but I couldn't wait another day. The campers don't stop throwing out their trash, you know."

As if Dad had called them, Lynn and Charlie's truck came through the gate. They pulled up next to Dad, who put a hand on the door to lean in the open window to talk. "How'd it go?"

Lynn smiled, although her eyes looked tired. "We're all set." Charlie asked her something, and she nodded. Lynn handed Dad a slip. "The people at the incinerator set up an account, and you can pay them monthly."

Stu laughed out loud. "They're your dumpster service? A woman and a little kid?"

Lynn's smile disappeared. Her eyes got suspicious.

"Who are you calling a little kid?" Charlie practically crawled over his mother to yell out the window. "I loaded lots of trash today!"

His mother hushed him. Roy snorted. "Kid's got spunk," he said.

"Charlie, you work so hard, you remind me of these three boys when they used to pick up the trash for me." Dad calmly tapped Lynn's door. "Go now. Thank you. For everything."

Lynn put the truck in gear, but she didn't take her foot off the brake. She turned to answer Dad, but her words were for Stu. "You tell Mr. Goodwin I'll come by tomorrow to talk, see if we can't work out a deal."

"You sure?" Dad asked. "You're kind of overloaded now. I'm afraid you won't find time to take care of everyone."

"I'm not afraid of hard work," Lynn said. "I actually kind of missed it these last six months, while I was traveling all over, looking for a job, and a place to live. I signed on two new customers today. I'll take more if they'll have me." With one last look at Stu, she slowly drove off toward her campsite.

Stu watched thoughtfully until Lynn's taillights were out of sight. He smoothed out the papers on his clipboard. He felt in his pockets and pulled out a business card.

Dad held up his hand in a stop-right-there way. "I told you—" my father began.

Stu interrupted. "She isn't in it for the long haul. She'll get a day job. The kid'll have to go back to school. Or they'll get tired of the back-breaking work. They'll cut corners and find ways to make the job easier. I've seen it all. Whatever. But you're going to need me." He held out the business card. "You're all going to need me at some point."

Dad waved the card off.

Stu pocketed the card, shrugged. "When you do, I'll be waiting." He put his pen in his shirt pocket, and with one last look at Dad, climbed up into his rusty old garbage truck. He turned the key, and the motor roared. Shifting, he looked over his shoulder to back up, and the truck died. Stu frowned. Pumping the gas a couple of times, he turned the key again, and the truck roared to life. With a *beep, beep, beep,* the truck backed up a little too quickly, before turning to roll out our gate.

Dad pulled off his hat to scratch his head. But I noticed he wasn't watching Stu leave.

He was looking toward Lynn's site.

Chapter 19

Bears will dig up an underground wasp nest and eat the insects, nest and all!

"Do you really think they'd do that to your dad?" Packrat asked, adjusting the backpack of tools he was lugging. "Do you think Lynn and Charlie would stop hauling your trash?"

"Help comes and goes for your parents," Roy said, hitching his own backpack higher on his shoulder as he led the way down the trail. "Well, except for the three of us, and Packrat's mom."

Packrat stopped and held out an arm. When we stopped, too, he pointed to a snake slithering across the path in front of us. It was brown, with a yellow ring around its neck and a light yellow belly. It moved silently and slowly, side to side, with its head raised and tongue poking in and out. We watched until it slid into the shadows of a pine tree, and out of sight.

"Cooool," Roy breathed.

Roy had woken up the same old friend we'd always known. All through our morning workload, he didn't seem to want to talk about his dad, or, as he now called him, The Traitor. When he'd used that name this morning in the store, my dad snorted, then coughed so hard Mom had to come over to hit him on the back like a little kid.

It only took a few more steps and we were at the fallen tree, where we took a left off the trail.

"Back to bathroom digging," Roy said. He dropped his backpack to the ground next to the dig site with a clang.

"Privy digging!" Packrat and I said.

"Same thing," Roy said with a shrug. "I dig first."

Packrat took a rope from his vest pocket and tied it to a tree, so we could use it for climbing in and out, and for lifting the buckets of dirt we'd be pulling out of the hole today. Roy unzipped the backpack and tipped it upside down so all the tools clattered to the forest floor. I dropped the small cooler and rake I'd lugged. Packrat went to collect the bigger tools we'd left in the bushes overnight.

The sun was almost straight above us, and the day was already hot. Everything was still.

Roy pulled off the privy's camouflage cover to drop a couple of trowels inside. Then he dropped in the buckets we'd left behind. He wasn't wasting any time today.

"I have a feeling," he called up to us as he climbed down the rope, "it's gonna be a good day."

Packrat followed him in. I knew it'd take a minute to fill the buckets, so I had a little time to kill. "I'm going to look around a bit," I said. Packrat nodded, already shaking the sifter back and forth over a bucket.

I walked past the cellar hole and over to the hand-dug well. *We should fill that up with rocks or something,* I thought. *Maybe rocks from the stone wall.* I'd get the guys to help me before we went home.

Climbing a little banking, I stopped to look around, trying to imagine the Wayside Inn standing right in this spot. People walking around in fancy clothes, the women in long dresses, the men wearing hats and holding canes. Horses and buggies coming and going.

As I turned around in a circle, a square stone caught my eye. Too square to be natural, it stuck out from a blanket of leaves. I put out a hand to pick it up, but realized it was much bigger than I thought. Longer, too. Kicking back years' worth of leaves and dirt that had settled around it, I discovered it was five feet long. Another lay above it. And a third. There were five in all.

These must be the steps leading nowhere that Game Warden Kate had talked about! I dug under the leaves a bit with my hands here and there, but I couldn't find any evidence of a wooden deck or brick-lined walkway. There was a really good view of the lake from up here, though. And blueberry bushes, lots and lots of them! No wonder we were seeing signs of bear all over the place. It was too early to pick them, but I'd have to remember to come back here in August. Blueberry muffins! Yum!

Something shiny caught my eye. I walked over, and there, lying on the ground, out in the open, was a soda can. Not a rusty, half-under-the-ground can, either. This one had been dropped within a couple of days because it didn't even look rained on. What the heck was it doing here? Packrat, Roy, and I always carried our trash out. I picked it up. Did we forget it?

Or had someone else been here?

Charlie?

"Cooper! Cooper!"

Packrat's cry wasn't a time-to-dump-the-buckets yell. It was more like a quick-we-found-something call! I ran down the banking. Dropping to my knees on the edge of the privy hole, I sent crumbles of dirt falling on my friends. I asked between breaths, "What'd ya find?"

Packrat looked up at me, a grin from ear to ear. Roy was still hunched over the sifter. I couldn't see what was in it.

"Gold?" I asked.

Roy looked up. "Nope. But . . ." He held up a small bottle, black in color. It was short, with six sides, a neck, and an opening that flared out.

"An inkwell?" I was disappointed for only a second. "Hey! That's a rare find!"

Packrat stood on his tiptoes to hand up the bottle. There were no markings, nor a cover. I'd have to research it some more later.

I put it in the "found" pile. Then I hauled up the buckets of dirt to dump them. Looking back into the hole, I realized my friends were pretty deep now. The sides of the privy hole towered over their heads by another two feet, and they slanted outward.

I wiped my brow with the back of my arm. It sure had gotten hot.

"Time for lunch," Roy announced. "Hand mine down?"

"You aren't going to eat up top?" I raised an eyebrow.

He shook his head. "It's way cooler down here." Turning over two of the buckets, he said, "Seats. Drop the cooler down and we'll have three. One for each of us." He looked at his hands, and I swear I saw him shudder. "Packrat? Do you still have any of that hand sanitizer stuff?"

"Good idea!" Packrat said, patting his pockets until he found it.

After they'd washed their hands, I tossed Roy's lunch to him, and dropped the little cooler down, too. Packrat took his own lunch out of one of his inner pockets. "Don't your lunches get squished in there?" I asked.

He pulled out a very flat, very soggy, peanut butter and jelly sandwich. "I like them that way."

I climbed down the rope, my lunch bag between my teeth. Sitting on the cooler, I washed my hands with some of my bottled water before opening my bag. I had a ham sandwich, a small packet of chips, and two cookies. Some kids might find it boring, but it was my favorite.

For a couple of minutes, all you could hear was us chowing down and slurping our drinks. "Hey," I said, remembering the can I'd left up on top, "either of you bring a can of soda with you the last time?"

They both shook their heads.

"I found one up on the hill behind the cellar hole. It wasn't rusted or anything."

Roy swallowed what was in his mouth. His eyes narrowed. "Someone else hanging around this hole? Looking for our gold?"

"I don't think so," I said, but Charlie's face popped into my head again, eyes wide when he'd heard what the blue bottle was worth.

Roy thrust his hand in his paper lunch bag, rustled it around a bit, then poked his face in it. Sighing, he crumpled it up into a little ball.

I grinned. "Want a cookie?"

His face brightened. "Sure!"

"You didn't even ask what kind!" Packrat teased.

"I never met a cookie I didn't like!" Roy said, as I tossed him one.

There was only three feet between us. I mean, our knees were practically touching in this hole. But still, Roy bobbled the cookie. It hit one hand, then the other, then his knees, until it fell into the dirt by our feet.

Packrat stopped chewing. His eyes got round.

Roy picked up the cookie, blew on it, wiped it on his pants, inspected it, then bit into it.

"Ewww!" Packrat cried.

"What?" Roy asked, taking another bite.

"We're sitting in a . . ." Packrat stopped.

I couldn't resist. I had to finish it. "Privy!"

There was exactly ten seconds of silence. As I watched, Roy's face turned green. Turning to the side, he spit into the corner of the privy hole over and over and over. Packrat and I doubled over laughing. Roy grabbed the sleeve of his T-shirt and wiped his mouth with it. "I forgot for a second!"

My stomach hurt. I could barely breathe. I fell off the cooler, laughing some more. Getting back up, I teased, "C'mon! The five-second rule works here, too."

"Not even a five-tenths-of-a-second rule works in a privy!" Packrat gave me a wink. Oh man, my friends knew how to get to one another.

"A one-hundred-and-fifty-year-old privy," I pointed out. "I think we can just call it a hole now."

"A privy once is a privy forever!" Roy started scrubbing his tongue with his T-shirt.

Packrat pulled some napkins out of his coat pocket, "Umm, you do realize your T-shirt is probably covered in dirt from digging . . ."

Roy's eyes looked like they were going to fall out of their sockets. He snatched the napkins from Packrat's hand, took a giant swig of water, then spit it out in the corner of the hole.

"I swear," he warned, "you two better not say nothin' to nobody about—"

Maaaaaaah! MAAAAAaah!

Molly? The scream sounded like a kid in trouble. Big trouble! The hair on the back of my neck stood up.

Maaaaaaah!

We jumped up from our seats, what was left of our lunches falling to the privy hole floor. Grabbing the rope, I climbed up until I could peek over the edge.

"What can you see?" Packrat whispered urgently. I shook my head, and he rummaged around in an inside pocket. Pulling out a small pair of binoculars, he handed them up to me.

I scanned the area. Nothing. Not even a moving shrub branch. Maybe we'd imagined it.

Maaaaaaah!

Crunching leaves and breaking twigs. As I scanned the area, I thought I saw . . . there! A flash of brownish-red! The kit again? No! The ears were all wrong. Short and rounded. A bear cub! It was racing, falling, twisting and turning. It cried out again. And again.

I climbed all the way out of the hole, Packrat and Roy right behind me. "Quick!"

Running for the cellar hole, I reached the shorter wall and put my elbows on the top. Packrat pulled another pair of binoculars from his coat and the two of us searched the woods again.

Packrat's gasp told me he'd seen the bear, too. Passing his binoculars to Roy, he pointed.

The cub had its head caught in the handle of a thick plastic grocery bag. Every time it rubbed at it with its paw, it made a crinkly noise that scared the cub. But when it tried to run from the bag, it stayed on its ear. The cub kept clacking, or popping, its jaws, which I knew meant it was scared. It swiped at the bag again, and when it didn't come off, the little bear opened its mouth and screamed.

"We have to help!" I stood up.

Packrat and Roy grabbed my shoulders to pull me down.

"No!" they said together.

And that was the very first time my friends had ever told me no.

Chapter 20

Predators of first-year cubs include birds of prey, foxes, bobcats, coyotes, and other bears.

I shrugged off my friends, who were trying to hold me back.

"What the heck?" I whisper-yelled. How could they tell me not to help the poor cub? Now, its head was stuck inside the plastic bag as it turned in circles, trying to get it off. "We have to help!" As if it agreed with me, the cub screamed like a kid again.

"Never, ever get between a bear cub and its mom!" Packrat stared me down, then went back to looking through his binoculars. "She's got to be out there somewhere!"

"With all the noise it's making, she'll come running any minute," Roy agreed.

My legs shook from the effort of not running over to the cub. It was only about a foot high; it couldn't be very old at all. Its snout was tan in color, which told me it was a black bear. Its fur, though, was reddish.

"Black bear moms will bluff-charge. They aren't that aggressive," I pleaded. "Well, rarely. But it's in trouble! We can do this!"

One handle of the bag was now twisted and tangled around the cub's front right paw. The other handle was twisted around its neck. No mother bear could free it from this tangled mess! The cub hopped on three paws a couple of times, then sat to try to pull its paw from the handle. This only made the bag tighter around its neck. Its cries were weaker and sadder by the minute.

"I've got to help," I said. "I can't watch this anymore. I don't know where the mom is; maybe she's watching us, watching her cub. But if she was gonna come out, she'd be here by now."

Packrat and Roy exchanged a glance.

"Okay," Packrat agreed. He pulled out his phone. "Just let me call the warden—" He frowned. "I forgot. No service here." Taking off his vest, he said, "Okay, let's do it."

I shook my head. "You don't have to. Just be lookout."

Roy laughed. "Yeah, right! And give you all the glory. Uh-uh. We want in, too."

Staying low, we slowly worked our way over to the cub, which was sitting and breathing heavily, its head still inside the bag. I wasn't sure if it even knew we were there, because it was so stressed out and tired.

When we got within five feet, I signaled Packrat and Roy to stop. Crouching down, I held out my hand for Packrat's vest. I noticed it was pretty dirty, dirtier than I'd ever seen his coat. We'd had so many rescues lately. The seagull. The fox kit. Something wasn't right, but—

I shook my head. I'd worry about that later. I had to save the cub first, before its mom got here. If its mom got here. Something wasn't right there, either.

Like all the other saves this week, I gently threw the vest over the cub, then backed up a couple of steps, and waited. It moved around for a second or two, then stopped. Packrat handed me some thick work gloves and I put them on while my friends crept over to hold the edges of the vest down.

Carefully, I pulled back one corner of the vest to expose the cub's right paw. I almost gasped to see how big it was! And those claws!

The cub squirmed a little. "It's okay, little guy," I whispered soothingly until it settled.

"Hurry up," Packrat insisted, one eye on the woods.

"I'm going as fast as I can," I whispered back in a singsong voice, trying not to scare the cub. "I have to twist off this handle—"

Roy reached around me with his utility knife, and using the scissors, cut the handle in one swipe.

I should've thought of that. I shot him a grateful look. Putting the paw back under Packrat's big vest, I took a deep breath and glanced at my friends.

Moving to the other side, I folded back the vest so I could get a good grip on other handle, where it went around the cub's head. Knowing there was nothing I could do to keep from frightening the cub, I decided to use the Band-Aid method. In one motion, I pinched the handle in my fingers and quickly pulled it up and back. Roy snipped it, I pulled it all the way off, and we scooted back away from the cub, Packrat pulling his vest away with him.

The cub's eyes blinked a couple of times. Its chocolate-brown eyes met mine. If a little bear could be grateful, this one was.

I kept backing up slowly, so as not to freak it out. The cub shook itself from head to toe, as if shaking off a bad dream.

None of us took our eyes off the cub.

Slowly it stood, almost like it was checking to make sure the bag was really gone. It huffed once, twice, then ran into the bushes.

"Whew!" Roy gave a half-laugh. "I don't know what you two were all worried about."

Packrat punched him in the arm. "And you weren't?"

"Nah!" Roy smirked.

I held up the bag and looked at it. It was your usual grocery-store bag. Two handles. Made from a thick plastic. Big enough to hold a watermelon. But it looked new. Dry.

And the name on it was Goodwin's General Store.

There were only two ways it could've gotten out here: One, someone brought it on purpose for some reason, like, they were on a hike and using it to carry stuff; or two, someone threw it out of a car window.

I didn't like either option.

I stood and started walking in the direction the bear cub had gone. Roy and Packrat followed.

"Something's going on," I muttered.

"Too many animals caught up in trash," Packrat agreed.

"Maybe it's just coincidence," Roy argued. "You know, like all of a sudden seeing ravens wherever you go because somebody you know has a pet raven."

We walked for maybe ten minutes before pushing through a set of young pine trees and coming to an old stone wall. I stopped, blinking several times because I couldn't believe what I was seeing.

Packrat gave a short, sharp bark of a laugh. "What were you saying, Roy?"

Before us was a cleared area, like a rectangular field. The stone wall went all the way around it. On the other side of the field and wall were more woods. Through the woods, leading into the field, was an old, overgrown, and unused driveway. I figured that it led out to the road Dad had told us about.

But the field wasn't the reason we'd stopped. It was the trash in the back left corner of the field. Not a fast-food-bag-tossed-out-a-car-window kind of trash. Not a trash-can-tipped-upside-down pile. More like three huge mounds' worth. As we stood on one side of that stone wall, ravens, seagulls, and crows flew down to peck at it, and a fox raced for the woods.

It looked like the dumps from the old days. Dumps I'd researched when writing my paper about the importance of recycling. Except these were three tall, wide piles of mostly bagged trash. Between and around the piles, there was a carpet of litter. Probably scattered by the wind and the animals pawing and pecking at it.

I'd seen a lot of trash-related things since we'd bought the campground. People writing on the bathroom walls I'd just cleaned. Kids dropping candy-bar wrappers right outside the camp store when there was a trash can only a couple of steps away. Dying fish left in the rental boats. But this? This made me so mad, I wanted to kick the wall. My fist opened and closed.

How could they?

"Who?" Roy whispered. "This is a lot of trash! From way more than one house."

"I bet—" Packrat hesitated.

"What?" I practically spat out the words.

"Well, you made a lot of people mad with your project, Cooper. Could it be payback?"

We walked over to the piles to get a closer look. They were mostly made up of trash bags of every color and size, some ripped open, some not. Here and there were more of the bags from Goodwin's General Store, too. In one spot, there was a whole bunch of rotten fruits and vegetables, like from a restaurant or store. Weird things stuck out from between the bags, too, like the sad face of a one-eyed teddy bear, a dirty Superman beach towel, a dog's cracked water bowl, and a pink, plastic flamingo with no legs.

Roy tugged a folding camp chair from the pile and set it up. "This is perfectly good! What are they thinking, throwing it away!"

"Again, who?" I threw my hands in the air. "It could be anybody!"

"Hey," Packrat exclaimed, "a clue!" He reached out to tug on an envelope sticking out from a ripped bag. "It's stuck." As he tugged, a rotten baby diaper came out with it. Packrat dropped that letter like a hot stone from the campfire.

"Ewww!" we cried as one.

"So much for that clue," Roy said. "I ain't touching it."

"Okay, okay," I said. "What do we know?"

Roy raised an eyebrow. "The dumpster owner guy, Stu? He kept telling your dad he'd need him sooner or later. Like a threat."

I nodded.

"And Mr. Goodwin was pretty mad," Packrat said to Roy. "You should have seen the look he gave Cooper in the town hall meeting. There are a lot of his bags here. The food could come from his lunch counter."

I kicked a can. "He couldn't have hauled this much trash all by himself. No one person or business would have this much."

"He's siding with all the other businesses that are fighting Talbot," Packrat pointed out. "All together, that'd be a lot of trash."

I shook my head. "Lynn went to see him. To sign him up—"

Roy raised an eyebrow. "So what about Lynn and Charlie? Your dad said she already had too many clients. Dropping the trash off here would mean she could pick up more trash in a day, 'cause she wouldn't have to drive all the way to the incinerator."

"I don't know," Packrat said, putting his hands in his pockets and staring at the trash.

Roy bent down to pick up one of Mr. Goodwin's bags, dangling it off his pointer finger.

I hated to admit it, but all our clues so far pointed in Lynn and Charlie's direction.

Chapter 21

Mother bears leave their cubs at "babysitter trees"
while they search for food. Cubs play at the base or
sleep on branches while waiting for her to return.

The walk back through the woods, the kayak ride to the camp-ground, the whole night in the tent on my front lawn—all we talked about were the suspects. The way we saw it, there were three: First, Mr. Goodwin and all his protesting friends, since there were a lot of his bags at the scene; second, the dumpster company guy, 'cause he was acting suspicious and telling my dad, in a bossy way, that he'd need to hire him to haul his trash sooner or later. And Mr. Goodwin's bags could be thrown away anywhere, even dumpsters. And third, Lynn and Char-lie. They were new in town, so they didn't know anybody, or have any connections to the area. They seemed to have more business than they could handle, so they might cut corners. And Mr. Goodwin's bags could be part of the trash that they collected from anyone, or anywhere.

But we had no proof that any of them were responsible. Not really; not yet. We suspected them because our guts told us to, but you can't accuse someone based on how your gut feels.

The next morning, we raked the campsites for the campers who were due to arrive that day. We checked the bathrooms and brought up bundles of wood to restock what we sold from the porch store. We worked double-time all day, making sure every last job was done, and done well, because we had a mission. And we needed time to accomplish it.

We were biking into town to see if we could find more clues.

Riding side by side down the driveway, we turned to ride single file on the sidewalk. Before she'd let me leave, I'd had to promise Mom a gazillion times I'd stick to it. In her long, crazy list of biking-into-town rules, this was the one she kept coming back to. Not stranger danger. Or being home before dark. It was staying on the sidewalk.

Now, as the three of us pedaled the three-mile stretch, Roy was really being a jerk. He insisted on riding beside the sidewalk, in the road. Every quarter-mile or so, he'd hop the curb to get in front of me on the sidewalk, then slow down until I had to pass him. Two minutes later, he'd hop off the sidewalk back into the road to ride beside me again. The first couple of times, I ignored him. But after two miles of this, my insides were all knotted up tight. I knew he was showing off, doing it on purpose. But why?

When we got to the school, we looked both ways and crossed at the crosswalk. Well, Packrat and I did. Roy, he crossed at an angle, missing it completely. Reaching the beginning of the rotary, we stopped.

The six farmhouses on the right side each had their barrels of trash out in front, but they were overflowing onto the ground. Several of the bags had been torn or broken into by animals.

"Wildlife has struck again," Packrat said, shaking his head.

"They've got barns! Why don't they store it in there?" Roy wondered.

Remembering all those angry looks at the meeting, I knew why.

"Warden Kate said they're leaving them out front for Talbot to see. Like a protest. That guy," I said, pointing to a man picking up loose trash blowing around at the end of his driveway, "he's a friend of Mr. Goodwin's. Eats at his place all the time."

We all looked toward the store we'd come to check on. There were three cars out front, which meant Mr. Goodwin had customers.

"Are we gonna walk in?" Packrat asked.

"And say what?" Roy scoffed. "Mr. Goodwin, are you dumping your trash on Cooper's property?"

"Well, we can't collect any clues from here!" Packrat insisted.

Cooper and Packrat: Mystery of the Bear Cub

"I think," I said, as I watched a fourth car park out front, "we should sneak around back."

We all pushed off to bike single file, with me in the lead. There was a dirt footpath that wound around behind the church to the tarred area behind it, the post office, and Mr. Goodwin's store. The real entrance was at the other end. People who worked and lived here knew to use this extra parking area when it got too busy out front. Visitors to town, or people passing through, tended to pull up out front.

Not having the transfer station open, I was worried there'd be a giant mess back here, like the one in front of the houses across the rotary. But when we rounded the corner, I slammed on my brakes, my back tire skidding to the side.

The dumpster behind the post office was overflowing, the cover not shutting all the way. But Mr. Goodwin still had regular trash cans. And they were neat and tidy.

I know he said he was trying to keep it clean because of the bear and her cub hanging around, but still. There were three possibilities. One, he was making the two-hour trip to the incinerator on his own, which didn't seem likely, since he ran the place from six a.m. to eight p.m. by himself. Two, he'd gone ahead and hired Lynn. Or three, he was dumping his trash on our property.

Mr. Goodwin, though? He was our friend.

But . . . he was a friend who was angry at Talbot. And yeah, at me, too. A little.

The screen door opened and Mr. Goodwin stepped out, a giant black trash bag in his hand. He walked down his back steps, letting the screen door slam behind him. I knew the minute he saw us by the dumpster, because he jumped a mile.

"Well, hello there." He moved toward one of the four cans lined up outside his store. Unhooking the bungee cord of the green one closest to him, he lifted the lid. "You don't usually hang around town after supper like this. Did your mom send you for milk?"

I shook my head. He put the bag in the can, replaced the lid, and stretched the bungee cord from one handle to the other. All the while, Packrat, Roy, and I stood with one foot on the ground, and the other on the pedal of our bikes. We'd come for clues, but I had no idea what I was looking for.

Mr. Goodwin turned to go back into his store, and I blurted, "What are you doing with your trash?"

He turned back around, his eyebrows going down into a low-dipping unibrow. "What?"

A low-throated rumbling sound poured from the woods on our left.

"Quick!" Mr. Goodwin yelled, opening his door. "Get in!"

We dropped our bikes, not because of the noise, but because of Mr. Goodwin's reaction. He made it sound like there were zombies or a dinosaur or a—

"Bear," he said simply, when we were all inside and safe.

I looked at him, and saw his face was etched with worry.

"She's still hanging around?" I asked.

"Dusk seems to be her favorite time of day to visit. She's a little early today, though."

The big black bear emerged from the woods before the last word was out of his mouth. She plodded toward the dumpster, walked around it, then stopped to put her paws on the cover. Grunting once, twice, she finally dropped on all fours to continue over to Mr. Goodwin's trash barrels. And not just any barrel, either. She went right for the one he'd just put the bag in. Swatting the can until it fell over, she sniffed it before biting the edges of the cover with her teeth.

"I just bought those!" Mr. Goodwin moaned.

Cooper and Packrat: Mystery of the Bear Cub

The bungee cord and cover popped off the can and the bear crawled inside. Packrat snickered to see her behind sticking out. When she wiggled it, I laughed, too. So did Mr. Goodwin.

Roy looked over the bear, into the woods. "So where's the cub?"

"Sometimes it comes out, but usually it waits by a tree just out of sight, until she drags something over."

Slam! A door opened and closed next door.

"Mary!" Before Mr. Goodwin could poke his head outside to warn her, we heard a little squeak of surprise, and the door slammed again.

"Mr. Goodwin!" called Mary, from the safety of the post office. I looked at the bear, which wasn't paying attention to any of us. "You've got to do something about your cans! Please, get a dumpster!"

"Told you, I can't afford it!" Mr. Goodwin hollered back. The lines on his face got deeper. "Besides, I saw this here bear and her cub get in your dumpster two days ago! Nothing's gonna stop them now that they've found an open-air diner."

When we didn't hear any response, Mr. Goodwin said, "She'll call Warden Kate." Hearing the tinkling of the bell at his own front door, he turned to go. "Stay here until the warden comes, or until the bear is good and gone," he warned before leaving.

It took ten minutes for the warden to show up. Not even the sound of her truck pulling into the parking lot made the bear go back into the woods. Warden Kate opened her door slowly, and got out carefully. Giving the bear a lot of space, she came to stand by the back door to talk to us. The bear looked at her only once before flipping over the fourth trash can with her paw.

"She's been here for about fifteen, twenty minutes," I said. "Mr. Goodwin's trash cans were all empty except for the one he'd just put a bag of trash into. But she's got to check every last one of them to be sure."

The warden watched the bear lean over a fallen can, then pull at the lid with her big claws.

"The bear's gotten used to Mr. Goodwin's routine; she knows by time and smell that he's put the bag out here. It's a problem all over town. Not everyone's been good about getting dumpsters or storing their trash or hauling it away," Warden Kate said.

"What are you gonna do?" Packrat nodded toward the bear.

The warden studied the animal. "I should probably relocate her. This parking lot always has cars coming and going. And once bears lock on to free food, they're pests. And dangerous ones at that. We call them habituated bears, or nuisance bears."

Cooper and Packrat: Mystery of the Bear Cub

"Wait! No!" Roy put up a hand, as if she was going to do it right that second. "Mr. Goodwin says there's a cub," he added, ducking his head. "Don't separate them. Please."

The warden looked thoughtfully at the bear, then at us. "A cub? Interesting. Mary didn't tell me that. Okay. I'll talk to Mr. Goodwin and see what we can do to frustrate the bear into looking elsewhere for food. This trash situation . . ."

I hung my head, and the warden put a hand on my shoulder. "That's not a complaint, Cooper. None of this is your fault. The town manager shouldn't have closed the transfer station. I personally believe he could have kept it open during the renovations. Now he's announced they need more time, two more weeks, to get it ready."

All three of us gasped. Another two weeks! No wonder everybody was so angry.

Warden Kate looked at the bear again. "Okay, so let's try this. I'll teach Mr. Goodwin a few tricks to discourage the bear and her cub— things like washing out all his cans and raking the area. I even have a few bear-proof trash cans I can let him try out. And we'll hope she moves along."

Warden Kate signaled to her assistant, who was sitting in the passenger seat of her truck. He stepped out with a metal trash-can lid and giant spoon.

"The old-fashioned way to scare off bears," she said, eyes twinkling.

"How many chances will you give her?" Roy asked softly.

"Two, because she knows there's food here and is bound to come back and try at least one more time. I'm hoping after two tries, and not getting food, and getting scared into leaving, she'll go back to living her life the way she was meant to live it."

"I could loan this to Mr. Goodwin," Packrat suggested, pulling an air horn from his pocket.

The warden smiled. "Great idea."

The big bear had her head back in the first can, the one with the bag of trash. Warden Kate shooed us back inside the screen door. Her assistant stood in the back of the pickup truck and, at a nod from the warden, he hit the lid with the spoon. The bear backed up so fast, she practically fell over trying to get out. When she was free of the can, she turned toward the sound and stood up on her hind legs.

"Yep, looks like she has one or more cubs." Warden Kate pointed to the bear's stomach, where teats showed through the fur. The warden looked into the woods. "It's probably hiding in there, up in a tree or behind the bushes."

"Won't this noise scare off the cub, too?" Packrat looked worriedly toward the tree line.

The bear plopped back on all fours and ran for the woods.

"It'll follow its mother," Warden Kate said.

Remembering the scared eyes of the cub we'd rescued in the field, I imagined the one in the woods here probably felt about the same.

"It's okay, little one," I whispered, imagining this cub up a tree, watching these humans scare its mother. "At least you have your mom to take care of you."

Chapter 22

*Male black bears weigh 250 to 600 pounds and are
five or six feet long from the tip of their nose to the tip
of their tail. Females are smaller, four to five feet long,
and weigh 100 to 400 pounds.*

After the bear had disappeared into the woods behind Mr. Good-win's store, we went back outside. Standing in the lot, we told Warden Kate about the trash dump we'd found on campground property.

"How much was there?" she asked. "Sometimes, people lose a bag or two when they blow out of their trucks—"

"Waaaaaay more than that," Roy said.

"More like two full dumpsters' worth," Packrat said, pointing to the one behind him. "Three, maybe."

The warden looked at me. "What are you thinking, Cooper?"

I scuffed the toe of my sneaker into the dirt, drawing a triangle. "I wish I'd never written that report."

The warden got down on one knee. "It's a great idea, Cooper. I'm telling you, it's the town manager who—" She sighed. "Never mind that. Just know it's not your fault. You think someone is doing it on purpose?"

"What else could it be?" I cried.

"I'll try to drive down and take a look at it as soon as I get a minute, okay? See if I can't find a clue."

Warden Kate's radio crackled. She pulled it off her belt to listen. Someone on the other end said, "We have a homeowner who says he has a bear in his yard, damaging his property. He wants to shoot it."

The warden rolled her eyes. "No shooting without a bear permit," she said firmly into her radio. "I'll be right there. Tell him we'll dart it this time. Relocate it.

"Sorry, boys—gotta go. That bear has had all its chances." Warden Kate climbed in her dark green pickup truck, her assistant getting back in the passenger side. She put the truck in drive.

"Cooper, the bears are hungry. Normally, I'd say they wouldn't chase you. Heck, they'd smell you coming a mile away and avoid you completely. But at a trash dump . . ." She shook her head. "They aren't going to act normally. Maybe you three should stay away from that location until I can be there with you. Which might take a couple of days. Okay?"

I nodded. But my fingers were crossed behind my back.

I didn't have to look to know Packrat's and Roy's were, too.

Overnight, we'd all made a pact to skip digging in the privy for one day, and instead clean up what we could in the field. I had no idea what I did to deserve these friends of mine. I mean, really? Nobody else I knew would exchange digging for buried treasure for digging in a smelly, slimy, fly-infested trash heap.

We'd talked to my dad, and he'd agreed to come by to pick up whatever bags we'd manage to fill, and haul away whatever dumped bags he could. "Besides, I want to see for myself what's going on over there," he'd said.

So when all our morning chores were done, we grabbed a roll of trash bags, gloves, some paper towels, hand sanitizer, and a couple of rakes. It was unanimous that we should take Roy's rowboat. He had a small motor on the back, so it would get us there in half the time.

After pulling the rowboat up on the little sandy beach, we gathered our tools and backpacks and headed up the trail to the trash dump. I'd promised Mom we'd be back in four hours, but I didn't tell Packrat and Roy. Lately, any rule-type promises I made to Mom or Dad seemed to make Roy annoyed with me. And if I got a shoulder squeeze or a compliment or, worst of all, a hug, from them, I heard about it for days. I really didn't get it. I think I'm the same friend, with the same family. We haven't changed. But suddenly, my family and the stuff we said and did was the butt of all his jokes. And the reason for his eye rolls. And his anger.

I'd asked Packrat about it last night, when Roy left the tent to get a drink in the house. He'd looked at me sadly and shrugged. "Yeah, I see it, too. I just wish he'd talk about it already so we could help him."

I did, too. Then maybe I'd get my friend back.

Now, Packrat stopped on the trail and looked to the left where our privy-digging site was. He sighed heavily. "Just a few more hours of digging, and I know we'd find something," he said.

Roy and I nudged him from either side, and he took the lead again. Roy walked behind him, and I was behind Roy.

"What's to stop the dumpers from doing it again, after we pick up this load of trash?" Roy asked.

Packrat opened one side of his vest as I answered. "I'm hoping that if they see we've cleaned it up, they'll know we know, and they'll stop doing it."

Packrat passed back a pair of heavy work gloves to Roy, who passed them to me. I took them from over his shoulder, adding, "Maybe they'll be afraid to come back, afraid to get caught."

Next came a pair of light brown gloves. Roy slipped them on, pushing down between the fingers of one hand with the other. "We can do this," Roy announced.

I wasn't sure if he was trying to convince us, or himself.

Birds chirped happily from tree branches. The rapid-fire sounds of a pileated woodpecker filled the air. Every now and then, we'd hear scurrying noises in the leaves under the bushes.

We rounded a corner and pushed through the saplings. Packrat gasped. Roy and I stepped up to the stone wall next to him. I looked down the left side of the field, bracing myself for the three mounds of trash we'd seen last time. I sucked in a breath. There were five piles now, all taller than us.

Roy groaned. "We can't clean up all of that!"

My friends' shoulders slumped as we climbed over the wall and walked into the field, toward the man-made mess. "Even if we managed to clear away one whole pile, I don't think they'd notice," Packrat said, picking up an old, stained, ratty baseball. "And the animals will still come for the rest. They'll paw at it and throw it all over the place. They'll keep getting tangled and caught. We'll never get ahead of the dumpers now. The jerks!"

"This is disgusting!" Roy declared. "Okay, okay, I admit—I never used to think about where my fishing line ended up if it broke and floated out of my reach, or got tangled in the weeds. But after seeing that poor seagull all twisted up . . ."

I put a hand on his shoulder. "For me, it's all the raking I have to do to make sure I get all the wrappers and soda cans and stuff off the campsites and the playground."

My friends were mad. And deep down, I was too. But mostly, I was sad. Sad that people would ruin the land this way. How would they like it if I dropped a broken bag of trash in the middle of their living room? Or a rotten apple core in their clean glass of water?

"We have to figure out who's doing this," I said. "But how?"

"We could camp out and stalk—" Packrat suggested.

I shook my head at him before Roy jumped all over the idea. Ever since the time we'd fooled our parents by pretending to stay in Packrat's tent, when we were really on a stakeout across the lake, our parents checked in on us during sleepovers. A lot. Especially my mom, who wouldn't be fooled twice. But I didn't want to say that out loud.

"What if we track the trash?" Roy looked thoughtfully at the mountain of it in front of him.

"Track it?" I asked.

Packrat rubbed his chin with his fingers. "Hmm. You mean, like put something in a Mainely Trash dumpster, and if it ends up here—"

"*Shhhh!*" I whispered. "I thought I heard—"

I put a hand on Packrat's shoulder and pointed to the other side of the pile. I could tell the second my friends heard the snuffling and snorting sounds, too, because their eyes widened.

We slowly tiptoed around the base of the trash heap. And there it was, at a second, smaller pile of trash about a hundred feet away.

The cub.

We got down low and watched. I wanted to shoo it away, but I knew that would only be a temporary solution. It'd just come right back the minute we left. Packrat took out binoculars and scanned the woods around us. No adult bears in sight. The cub pulled and pawed and worked at a clear plastic bag. I could tell it smelled something it wanted, because once the bag was open, it pushed rotted food aside to keep digging. When a jar of jelly rolled from the bag, the cub almost looked like we did when we scored one of Mr. Goodwin's warm doughnuts. The snorts and snuffles got louder. Happier. No doubt this little one was hungry.

"Where's its mother?" I muttered.

"Maybe she died," Packrat said, lowering his binoculars. "Does the male help raise them, too?"

The cub tried to put its nose inside, but the short round jar kept rolling away.

"No," I said. "The female gives birth during hibernation and when they come out in the spring, she teaches it all it needs to know to survive. The dad doesn't help at all."

Roy gave a short, quick laugh. "Reminds me of someone."

The cub slapped its paw on the jar, and this time it stayed. Sniffing the open end first, it then stuck its long, pink tongue inside once, quick. Licking its lips a couple of times, I swear I heard sounds that sounded like *yum.*

I couldn't help it. I smiled.

The cub licked that jar in earnest, trying to get every bit of leftover jelly it could.

SNORT! Grrrgh!

On the right side of the field, a big, big black bear came running out of the woods. Well, it was more like a slow jog. Packrat and Roy and I held our breath.

"The mother?" Packrat wondered out loud. Roy looked around wildly, and made a grab for something in the nearest trash pile.

"A baseball bat?" I asked.

He smacked it into his other hand. "In case it charges us."

I didn't think the bat would be a lot of help. But I didn't say anything.

Staying crouched low, we waited. The cub was so busy trying to get every bit of jelly it could, it never looked up. It never heard the big bear coming. Never heard it slowly walk the last few feet.

"It's the male," I whispered to my friends. "The one with the toilet paper? See the notch in its ear?"

"And the patch of white on its chest!" Packrat added.

The bear made a low rumbling sound, almost like thunder in the distance.

The cub did hear that. It scooted back, looking up fearfully. The big bear lifted a paw and before I could call out a warning, he swatted the little one. All three of us gasped as the cub rolled a couple of feet. Then we breathed a sigh of relief when it stood, shaking its head in a what-just-happened kind of way.

"What a bully," Roy said. Seeing the big bear pull the jar toward him and practically lay on top of it, I had to agree with him.

The cub gave a sad little pleading sound and went down on its belly. It slowly crawled back toward the jelly jar.

"Is it crazy?" Packrat cried. "There's all kinds of trash that it can choose from!"

Roy shook his head sadly. "This is not going to end well for Red."

"Red?" I whispered. Actually, I liked the name. It fit.

The cub crept forward some more. When it was close enough, it reached out a paw toward the prize.

The big bear turned his whole body, taking the jar with him. Red circled around to try again.

"Back away," Packrat urged. "It's not worth it!"

The big bear twisted back toward the little one and growled loud and clear for all the world to hear. This jar was his, and his alone.

The little bear stopped crawling, but didn't run. It eyed the jar.

Roy half-laughed. "He's a fighter."

"He's gonna get killed!" I said.

"I can't look!" Packrat put his hands in front of his face. But I saw him spread his fingers to peek.

Red put out a paw. The big bear swatted him again, throwing him several feet.

The cub lay still.

We all held our breath.

Get up, get up, get up! I pleaded in my head.

Slowly, Red stood. Shaking itself, the cub slowly walked away, looking back only once.

That was a close one.

Chapter 23

Female black bears can produce milk for their cubs in the den while hibernating, even though they won't have had water and food for weeks, or even months, before the cubs are born.

After the big black bear got bored with the jelly jar and left the scene, we did, too. We didn't even try to pick up any of the trash. What was the point?

And besides, we had a new plan.

The minute we stepped out of Roy's boat and back onto our campground dock, I called the office to have Mom tell Dad not to go to the field. We hadn't bagged any trash after all.

Mom said, "Thank goodness you called!" Which was code for "I've got some jobs for you to do that can't wait until your next work shift." And there were three. The ladies' room, middle stall, needed toilet paper. It was past time to test the pool. And could someone rake Site 23 for a camper who'd just called and would be checking in today?

Packrat, Roy, and I did Rock, Paper, Scissors to choose jobs, and agreed to meet back at the fire circle in half an hour with our bikes.

We did it in half the time.

I rolled up and parked next to my friends. "Got the trash we're gonna plant?" I asked.

Roy patted his backpack. I could see the handle of the baseball bat he'd found sticking out of the top, a big chip taken out of the end of the handle. Packrat pulled the stained and ratty baseball from his vest pocket. One seam was ripped wide open. These two pieces of equipment had seen a lot of games before someone had thrown them away, and they had marks that made them unique. Since none of us wanted to toss our own things in the dumpster and risk losing them forever, we'd decided to use these.

"Where are you guys going?"

Packrat quickly tucked the baseball in his pocket. I turned to find Charlie rolling down the window of their parked dump truck, while his mom walked into the store.

"Just a bike ride. Into town," I said.

"Oh." Charlie leaned forward so his whole upper body was out of the window. "I thought maybe you were gonna do more bottle digging."

I shook my head. "Not today. We, umm . . ."

"Had too many chores to do," Packrat half-fibbed.

"Gonna go later?"

As I shook my head no, I couldn't help but wonder: Was he asking because he wanted to go with us? Or could it be that he wanted to know when we *weren't* going to be there?

Then I thought, *I'm just letting my imagination run away with me.*

"My mom says you're trying to figure out who's dumping trash on your land." I swear, this kid had talked more in the last five minutes than he had since he'd arrived. "Any clues?" Charlie wasn't really looking at me. He was drawing in the dust on the door.

I glanced at my friends. Roy was staring at Charlie, like he was trying to read his mind, while Packrat's eyebrows were raised. Okay, so it wasn't just my imagination.

All of a sudden, Charlie scrambled out of the truck window, head-first. Twisting to land on his feet, he yelled to someone behind me, "Hey! Stop! Whoa!"

A car was driving toward us, a little too fast for campground roads. Charlie started running toward it. His arms were waving in the air. Lynn came rushing out of the store, yelling at him to stop, but Charlie kept on going. I could see that the lady in the car wasn't looking out the window, though. She was looking down, fiddling with her phone or the music or something.

"Charlie!" I yelled. Packrat and Roy started yelling, too. Lynn was yelling, and even my mom was hanging out the store window, yelling.

But Charlie didn't slow down.

It all seemed to happen in slow motion. Charlie ran in front of the car, bent over, and with one hand scooped something up out of the road. He took one step, two steps, then launched himself into the edge of Mom's pond garden, just as the car passed where he'd been standing. It wasn't until then that the lady saw him, and slammed on her brakes. I swear, the whole campground went still for half a minute.

Then everyone started yelling at once.

I rushed over with Packrat and Roy. There, in Charlie's outstretched hand, was Oscar.

Charlie had saved my three-legged frog!

I gave him a one-armed hug, while Roy clapped him on the back, and told him that was the most awesome rescue ever! Packrat explained to the lady in the car that Charlie had just saved the camp-ground's pet frog from getting flattened by her tires. The lady shook her head and said, "Maybe you should put up a frog crossing sign!" before driving out of the campground. Although a little more slowly, this time.

I took Oscar and gently slid him back into the pond. I'm pretty sure I saw him breathe a sigh of relief.

Only Lynn didn't look happy. In fact, she looked like she was the one who'd almost gotten run over. Grabbing ahold of Charlie's shirt, she tugged him back toward their truck. Halfway there, though, she stopped, hugged him tight, then let him go to talk his ear off all the way to the truck.

"What were you thinking?" Lynn's voice floated back to us. "You could have been hit by that car!"

"I don't know," Charlie said, scratching his head. "I didn't really think. The frog was gonna get squished. Cooper's frog."

Roy scoffed. Leaning over so only I'd hear, he said, "She's as bad as your mom."

I saw Lynn yawn as she turned to climb in the truck. I heard her say something about not sleeping well lately, and needing a nap before they went back out after supper to take care of more customers, and how Charlie's almost-accident had wiped years off her life.

Charlie crawled up in the passenger seat and asked a question I couldn't hear. Lynn shook her head no and Charlie slumped down, obviously pouting as his mother put the truck in drive and drove to their campsite. I sighed. It couldn't be them. Could it?

Could a frog rescuer and his mom be illegally dumping trash on our property?

Chapter 24

Usually shy animals, black bears can be scared away with loud noises—unless, of course, they've gotten used to humans and the noises they make.

Right after Lynn and hero Charlie drove to their campsite, we rode out of the campground gate and down the camp driveway on our bikes.

"You guys really think this is gonna help us catch the trash dumper?" Roy asked.

Packrat, who was in the lead, looked back at us over his shoulder. "Are you kidding? It's brilliant!"

As we rolled along the sidewalk into town, my friends and I went over the plan. We'd marked both the old, dinged-up bat and the ratty baseball with our initials, just on the off chance there would be other dinged-up bats and ratty baseballs in the newest piles of trash. We were going to put the bat in the Mainely Trash dumpster by the post office. The ball would go in Mr. Goodwin's trash, the cans Lynn and Charlie picked up. Whichever piece of equipment showed up at the trash dump would identify the bad guy.

Roy slowed down to ride next to me. "So, why didn't we just put one of them in your dumpster?"

I slammed on my brakes, and smacked my hand to my forehead. Packrat and Roy both swerved sideways and stopped to look back at me. "That was dumb!" I laughed at myself as I pushed off to join my friends again. "One hundred and thirty-two sites I could have thrown that ball into, to see if Lynn was the one we're looking for. Guess I keep forgetting we don't haul our own anymore."

"So what if neither one of these shows up in the next trash pile at the field?" Packrat swerved back and forth on the sidewalk in front of me as he talked.

"Then it's probably some of the other businesses in town," I replied. "They did get together to fight Talbot. Maybe they got together to haul their trash away, too."

Roy gave a short, quick bark of a laugh. "Wouldn't my father love that! The good guys in all this becoming the bad guys!"

"It's not them," I said quickly. I didn't want Roy's mood to turn dark again. Whenever it did, I got the worst of it. "I'm telling you, it's Mainely Trash."

"I'm betting on Lynn and Charlie," Packrat said softly.

"Whoa!" Roy stopped pedaling and slowly stood up on his pedals. "Is that . . ."

A shiny, electric-blue garbage truck drove toward us going in the other direction. As it passed, we saw Stu at the wheel. He smiled and waved at us.

"New truck," Packrat commented. "Business must be good."

Too good, I thought.

We pedaled past the library and the school. Instead of going straight down Main Street to the front door of Goodwin's General Store, Packrat took a left to follow the dirt path to the parking lot behind the buildings. I stopped behind the post office. Roy pedaled right up to the dumpster and lifted the lid, tossing the bat inside. It clattered to the empty bottom. Stu must have just been here. Darn. He probably wouldn't pick up the trash for a couple of days now.

We then rolled over to Mr. Goodwin's row of trash cans and stopped next to the closest one.

"Hurry up!" I urged Packrat, as he dug in a pocket for the ratty, old baseball.

"What you boys got there?"

All three of us jumped and turned back to see Mr. Goodwin standing at his screen door. He stepped through, and I saw he was lugging a bag of trash in one hand. Just your average black bag, nothing special we could track.

Packrat held up the baseball. "Umm, I found this ball. You know, on the side of the road—"

At the exact same time, Roy said, "It was mine, but I don't want it anymore."

Really? *Really?* My friends weren't very good at this sneaking-around stuff. "What they mean is," I explained, "Packrat found it on the side of the road—"

"And I wanted it," Roy butted in.

"But when he saw how used-up it was—"

"I didn't want it anymore," he finished.

Mr. Goodwin looked from one of us to the other and back again. When he opened his mouth to ask another question, I blurted out the first thing that came into my mind: "So what do you think about the new Mainely Trash garbage truck?"

That distracted him all right. Mr. Goodwin scowled and pointed a finger at me. "Do you know he bought that fancy-schmancy truck with all these honest folks' hard-earned money?"

I took a step back, even though I knew Mr. Goodwin wasn't mad at me this time.

"Stu just spent twenty minutes telling Lynn and Charlie all about it! It lifts the dumpsters with front forks on arms, and empties them into the back of the truck. And it has a remote-control arm to grab trash cans and dump them too! That man doesn't even have to get out of his truck now! Pshaw!"

I looked at my friends with a what-did-I-just-get-us-into look.

"He called it a . . . a . . . prototype. They've only made a hundred in the whole country, and he managed to get his hands on one. Lynn sure seemed impressed that it could do both kinds of dumping." Mr. Good-win pointed to his trash cans. "Me, I told him he'd never haul *my* trash!"

He smiled a little. "Actually, I would've liked to see him try to dump this new one. Could one of you boys put this bag of trash in there?"

I took it from him. "No problem!" Glad to see his angry story was done, I took the bag over to the new, round trash can. It was dark green, and stood four feet tall with two metal handles on top of the cover. The plastic looked pretty solid, like our pool chairs at the camp, only thicker. I tried to lift the lid off, like we did with the metal ones at camp, but it wouldn't budge. I put the bag down and tried to pull it up and off with both hands. Still, it wouldn't give.

Packrat came up beside me. "Try pulling or turning the handles on the top," he suggested. But still, it wouldn't open for us. Roy joined in, suggesting maybe there was a latch somewhere. A clip?

I tried twisting it off, like a soda bottle top, and still it didn't open. "I just want to give this can a good swift kick!" I said. "I give up!"

"I hope the bears do the same thing!" Mr. Goodwin chuckled. Folding his arms across his chest, he looked all pleased with himself. "This is my new bear-proof can. Go ahead. Beat on it."

I hesitated, but Roy sure didn't. "Bear-proof? We'll see about that!"

He tipped the can on its side and stood on it. Rolling back and forth on it like a log in water, he grinned from ear to ear. "No way a bear's getting in here!"

"You don't have claws," Packrat pointed out.

"And you don't weigh four hundred pounds," I added.

Mr. Goodwin chuckled. "Fair enough." He came over and stood the can up again. "But the bear has tried once already and failed." Putting his hands on either side of the can's lid, he pushed in two buttons, one under each hand, then twisted the top off. "Almost like a medicine bottle," he explained.

He started to lift the bag, but I quickly grabbed it. "I'll get it for you."

Packrat passed me the ball, out of sight of Mr. Goodwin. I lifted the bag, and dropped both the bag and the ball into the can.

"It's got a double wall to make it stronger, and to help keep the smells inside. And wheels to roll it anywhere I want," Mr. Goodwin was saying.

"Did the warden bring this one?" I asked.

"No, she's been too busy to get back over here. So I went ahead and used some of my savings to try this one out. They're expensive. I could only afford this one." Mr. Goodwin checked the latch. "But it's worth it, I tell you! That poor bear came back once and tried to get inside, but couldn't! This can is all it was promised to be!" Someone from inside his store called for him. "I've got to get back to the lunch counter. See you boys later."

The door slammed shut behind him. My friends and I looked at each other with wide eyes. "That was a close—"

Suddenly, we heard the snuffling noise we knew so well. There, half in and half out of the woods, was the adult bear. I searched, but I didn't see the cub with her. Remembering she only had two chances with Warden Kate, I groaned. "She couldn't get in the trash can, so why is she back?"

But the bear didn't go for the can. She started toward the dumpster. Packrat pulled his phone from his pocket and looked at me with questioning eyes. I scanned the buildings. No one was looking.

We should call.

Warden Kate would want us to call.

Roy shook his head. "Don't. Please." He gave us a pleading stare. "Let's shoo her away. Give her an extra chance. The can is working!"

"Okay," I said, before I could change my mind. "Ready, then? One, two, three!"

We ran at the bear as one, arms in the air to make us look bigger than we were. The bear snorted when she saw us, hesitated, then turned and ran back into the woods.

Roy hummed a little as we got back on our bikes. Packrat and I exchanged worried looks behind his back.

I wasn't sure how many more chances we should give this bear.

But I was pretty sure Roy would not forgive me if I called Warden Kate to come and get her.

Chapter 25

Black bears can run thirty miles an hour in short bursts.

The Fourth of July arrived, and every site in the campground filled up. Motorhomes, trailers, tents, and popups everywhere! Kids of all ages, from all over the country, gathered on the playground to swing and talk, or on the playing field to shoot hoops or play Ultimate Frisbee. Tons of people meant tons more bathroom cleanings, beach raking, pool vacuuming, and wood stocking. Packrat, Roy, and I were so busy, we didn't get over to the privy dig site for three more days. Which meant we didn't get to see right away if our little experiment had worked.

But where there's a will, there's a way. Cleaning bathrooms at eight in the morning so all the campers see sparkling sinks, showers, and toilets as they get ready for the day is one of the most important jobs we do, according to my dad. But when the camp is full, we don't finish until nine-thirty because all those campers keep interrupting us. By then, it's almost time to do all the other daily jobs. But Packrat, our night owl, came up with a brilliant plan!

Last night, we'd snuck out of the tent at one in the morning when the campground was dead quiet, and we cleaned those bathrooms top to bottom. There were no campers hanging around, asking us if we could step out so they could use it. Well, except for one kid, who we think was sleepwalking, because he walked straight to the stall and back out again without even looking at us.

So in the morning, while all the other kids our age were sleeping in, we were up and on the lake before the sun had cleared the tree line. Packrat muttered something about not thinking his one-in-the-morning idea all the way through. But I think he was sleep-paddling again.

We passed under an eagle, perched on the branch of an old pine tree, looking down on us like it was a king and we were its subjects. Its mate soared past, gliding just above the glass-like surface of the lake, before turning upward to softly land on the nest. Two brown-colored eaglets cried for their breakfast. Seeing the eagle's empty talons, I knew they'd be waiting a little longer.

Our paddles made the only ripples in the water. Packrat and I sipped our steaming hot cocoa, while Roy gulped his coffee. Without letting him see me, I looked at Roy over the rim of my travel mug. Every day since he'd told his dad he wouldn't visit him in Portland, his mom had passed messages along to Roy that said things like, "Please call; I'd like to explain. Hope you're catching a big fish. Love, Dad." Mr. Parker was even calling the camp office looking for Roy, because every other day, my mom handed him messages, too. But Roy wasn't budging. He was staying mad.

Packrat and I had tried dangling bets in front of him. How far could Oscar hop? Who could climb the highest in the old maple tree at the edge of the playground? My favorite was who could eat the most s'mores at the campfire. He didn't even nibble at any of them. And that worried me. Roy never, ever turned down a bet. Especially one that involved chocolate.

As we reached our landing spot, the sun rose up over the treetops to beam down on the lake, bathing it in a golden light.

We pulled our canoe up into the bushes and peeled off our life jackets. We were all wide awake now with the thought of finally figuring out who was dumping trash on my family's property.

I took the lead, quickly finding the trail. Behind me, my friends easily kept pace.

"Cooper." Packrat's voice was hushed, like the forest around us. "I almost forgot. I was in the store yesterday, getting an ice cream, and I heard the chip delivery guy telling your mom that Lynn and Charlie are really falling behind. They're not just missing their pickup times—they're late by days."

Cooper and Packrat: Mystery of the Bear Cub

I'd heard all about it over dinner. Mom and Dad had talked about nothing else. Dad wanted to meet with them, and help them figure out a plan to get caught up. Mom told him to have patience. They were doing their best; they'd just taken on too many accounts. She pointed out that even Mainely Trash wasn't sticking to their schedule. She thought that once the town's transfer station opened up again, some of Lynn's homeowner customers would go back to hauling their own trash. With fewer customers, Lynn would be able to get back on track. Dad replied that he'd heard the transfer station wasn't going to open on time—that Talbot was keeping it closed for a fourth week because the people building it had taken the Fourth of July weekend off and it still wasn't ready yet. Back and forth my parents went, until finally they agreed: Dad would just offer to help, see what they need, and go from there.

We walked past the bottle dump, then took a detour to the privy dig site. Lifting the camouflage cover, we looked inside. Everything seemed to be the way we'd left it.

"Sure wish we could dig for the gold," Roy said. He kicked a pebble and watched it roll over the edge to plop on the privy hole floor. "I just know it's there!"

Packrat nodded. "Just another couple of feet, I bet."

"C'mon," I urged, before I changed my mind and stayed to see if they were right.

Another ten minutes or so and I could see patches of green field through the trees. We half-walked, half-crawled toward the stone wall at the edge of it, listening carefully for anything human—or animal. The last thing we wanted to do was run into that mean bear, although a part of me hoped we'd catch the bad guys in action.

"Coast is clear," Roy said. He sounded almost disappointed.

Standing, I scanned the field and counted at least three more mounds of trash. My head had known they'd be there, but my heart had hoped they wouldn't. I sighed heavily.

We crossed over the rock wall, and turned left toward the newest mounds of trash at the end of the field. A raven, keeping watch at the top of a mound, was the first to spy us. Giving a shrill call, it warned the others, who took to the air with their prizes, echoing the call. Their alarm warned a coyote and a raccoon that silently raced for the trees in opposite directions.

Without speaking, we each claimed a pile. Any other adventure, we might have taken bets over who'd find the ball or bat. Or maybe played Rock, Paper, Scissors for first and second pick, with the loser getting the smelliest mound of trash. But I figured if Roy didn't want to have a s'more-eating contest, he wasn't going to care which pile he got.

Looking up at the top of mine, I shook my head. "We're crazy!" I muttered to myself, lifting up a tire and rolling it aside to look under it. "This is like finding an endangered northern leopard frog in a giant marsh. Impossible!"

Twenty minutes later, sweat was rolling down the sides of my face and the back of my neck. I wanted to wipe it away, 'cause it itched, but who knew what was all over my gloves! The pile was smelly, and while it was mostly bagged trash, there was loose stuff mixed in, too. Like a box of moldy oranges, and fast-food bags with half-eaten burgers inside. When Roy had put on the nose clip he'd brought when we'd first started privy digging, Packrat and I had laughed at him. But who was laughing now? He might look weird, but he wasn't gagging while trying to breathe.

"Found it!" Roy called. I jumped up to go look, but then I heard him say, "Wait. No." I peeked around my mound of trash and watched him toss a dented Wiffle ball to the top of his pile. When it rolled all the way back down to his feet, he sighed.

I kicked aside a clear bag that seemed to have all recyclables in it. "This is nuts. Maybe I should just go to Talbot," I said. "Beg him to drop this whole mess." Spying what I thought was the end of the bat, I yanked it out with one pull. But it was only an old wooden pole.

"Hey! Got it!" Packrat jumped off his pile.

"Yes!" Roy said at the exact same time. "Found it!"

I stood between them, my arms out wide. "You can't both—"

Packrat held up the ratty baseball like a hard-won trophy and turned it so I could see our initials. "We got proof! So I was right, it is Lynn and Charlie. Wait." He looked to Roy. "What?"

Roy lifted the chipped bat and stood like he was waiting for Packrat to throw the ball over home plate. "Our initials are on it."

I was so confused! My mind swirled with questions. "What does this mean? Are they in on it together? What the heck! Has the whole town gone crazy?"

"Wait, wait, wait. Let's think about this," Packrat said. He tossed the ball up in the air and caught it. "So Mr. Goodwin's trash is picked up by Lynn and Charlie."

Roy slapped the bat into the palm of his hand. "And the post office dumpster is emptied by Mainely Trash."

"Maybe the bear got in the bear-proof can, and the ball rolled out?" Packrat suggested, but I could tell he didn't buy it.

"What if Mr. Goodwin opened the can to put another bag in, but knocked it over and the ball rolled out?" I was reaching for an explanation here, but it couldn't be both Mainely Trash *and* Lynn. Could it? "Then someone came along, picked up the ball, and threw it in the dumpster."

My friends' faces told me they weren't convinced about that any more than I was.

"We've gotta try again," Roy said. "My science teacher says all good experiments are double-checked, right?"

"No digging again today?" Packrat almost pouted.

I shook my head. "Let's test this one more time." I turned to walk off the field. "We'll just pick the one that seems most logical. The dumpster—"

Rooooooooar!

We whipped around. The big male bear came running from the tree line on our left, as the cub bolted out from between the trash piles. It scampered right in front of us, eyes wide. The minute the cub slipped into the woods on our right, the male stopped running. Huffing and puffing, it seemed to say, *That's right. Run away. This is mine. All mine!*

We didn't stick around, either. Fast-walking to where the cub had disappeared through an opening in the stone wall, we stood still, listening.

"I'd like to get another look at it," I whispered.

"It looked smaller than I remember," Roy said.

"Thinner," Packrat agreed.

There. It was faint, but I heard heavy breathing. Scraping, like something sharp across a board. Walking forward, slowly, we made sure not to step on branches that would crack or leaves that would crinkle. We stopped. And again I heard the heavy breathing.

Over my head.

We looked up, and there was Red, lying on a tree branch and clutching it with its paws. The cub looked down at us with curious eyes.

"It's not running away," Packrat mused.

"I think it's too tired. Weak." I stepped back to get a better look, as Packrat fished around in his pockets.

Red made a whining noise and began licking one front paw with a long pink tongue. Up until now, it hadn't sat still long enough for us to get a good look at it. The cub had a light brown muzzle and dark brown eyes. There were a few little whiskers coming from either side of its nose, almost like a kitten. Its paws were huge, the pads on them hair-less, with all five claws sticking out. Tucking one of those claws under its chin, it closed its eyes. The run-in with the male bear must have taken all its energy if it could sleep with three humans standing under it. I smiled. If I tried that, I'd roll off the branch in my sleep for sure.

"It'd probably be in worse shape, if it didn't have the dump to feed from," I admitted. "But it's getting weak. And what if something bigger comes along and thinks Red is a meal?"

Roy's eyes were sad. "So it's abandoned. Isn't it? We would have seen the mother by now, if she was around."

"Yeah." I hated to admit it. "But maybe not abandoned, like the mother *wanted* to leave it alone. Maybe she was poached and can't come back. Or injured. We should call Warden Kate when we get back. See what she wants to do."

"The one thing I know," said Roy, his voice low, serious, "is that animals in the wild make way better parents than my dad does."

"Not all of them. He could be like a lion," I said with a grin. "They lie around all day while the female does the hunting and takes care of the kids and—"

Uh-oh. Roy's eyebrows went down, his look steely. The words had come out of my mouth before I'd thought about them. I'd forgotten for a minute that my friend's emotions had been all over the place lately. The Roy I knew would normally have laughed at my joke and come back with another.

But now, I swear I could feel the heat of his rising anger. I took a step back, nervous about the silence between us right now.

"So, hey, your dad is a good dad. He's just busy all the time. And you know, there are plenty of bad parents in the animal kingdom. Cruel, even. Eat-their-young kind of parents." I was babbling, and I couldn't stop. "The cowbird lays its eggs in other birds' nests, doesn't even hatch their chicks at all! Abandons them totally!" I was saying all the wrong things.

"Blueberries!" my friend cried, pulling a baggie from his pocket. But Roy and I ignored him, eyes on each other while Packrat became

the babbler. "I brought them in case you thought we should try to catch—"

"You have no idea what a bad parent is," Roy said, clenching his fists. "Or how it feels to have one."

"What the heck is *that* supposed to mean?" I looked to Packrat who shrugged. I turned back to Roy. "Your dad is not bad. There are worse things than having a father who works a lot!" *Or who isn't home.* But I couldn't say that last part, because he hadn't told us.

Packrat put a hand on his arm. "Roy, I know your life isn't perfect right now, but—"

Roy shrugged it off. "You guys know nothing. Nothing!"

"Then why not tell us?" I said. "We know something's going on."

"Because you wouldn't understand! Everything in your little world is perfect: perfect family, perfect life!" Roy ran his hand over the top of his head. His voice was angry, but his eyes were full of grief. "You work together, play together. Everybody loves everybody!" He stared me down again. "I'm sick of watching it!"

Packrat gasped. "Aw, c'mon, Roy. That's not fair."

"You and your mom are close! Even Charlie, who hasn't got a place to call home, has a mom who's there for him!"

Now I could feel my own anger brewing in the pit of my stomach.

"So *that's* why you've been mad at me? Because my family looks perfect to you? Are you totally forgetting that first summer we bought the campground—how my dad worked all the time?" I poked my finger into Roy's chest with every word. "We talked it out, worked on it! But there was a lot of yelling and mean words first. My life isn't always perfect."

"Coop, stop!" Packrat tried to worm his way in between us, but Roy took a step closer. "C'mon, you guys," Packrat begged. "We should be talking, not fighting!"

His words flew by me, but I didn't hear them. Afterward, when I'd calmed down, I wished I had listened. But in the here and now, in the heat of anger, I said, "If you can't stand watching my family and me, then don't look!"

Roy looked like I'd punched him in the nose.

And I felt like I had.

Packrat finally worked his way between us. "We need to talk," he pleaded. Looking to Roy, he added, "We can help. But you have to let us."

Roy took a step back. He shook his head.

"I'll paddle back with you guys. But then I'm done." He handed the bat to Packrat. "I quit this adventure."

CHAPTER 26

In some parts of the world, bear paws are considered medicine, which is just one of the reasons why poachers hunt bears.

For the whole trip back to the campground, none of us said a thing. A thousand apologies ran through my head, but not one of them reached my lips. I was mad, too. Sure, my family was close. Now. But I had rules I had to follow. Rules like only one piece of junk food a day. Roy could eat whatever he wanted, whenever he wanted. I had a curfew: home by ten o'clock sharp, or I was grounded. Roy went back to his campsite whenever he felt like it. I couldn't be on the lake after dark. Roy could fish for hornpout under a full moon.

And he was jealous of me? I think he just wanted to be mad at someone, and since his dad wasn't here, he was picking on me.

When we docked at the campground, Roy stormed off.

"Roy—stay!" Packrat called. He looked at me. "Talk to him!"

I shook my head. "You know Roy. He needs to cool off and think about it." I had some of my own thinking to do, too.

I locked up the canoe while Packrat took the gear. As we walked back to my house, he sighed.

"Let's pedal into town, drop the bat in the dumpster, then come back here and find him. But Cooper, I think something else is going on. Bigger than his dad working for Talbot. Bigger than Roy wanting more time with his dad."

Of course, he was right. "Yeah." I hoped by the time I got back, we would both be ready to talk.

Cooper and Packrat: Mystery of the Bear Cub

As Packrat and I rolled into the parking lot behind the church and post office, I stood on my pedals to look around. No one in sight. We rolled quietly and slowly forward. Closer. And closer.

"Be right back!" The voice came from inside one of the buildings. *Mr. Goodwin!*

"Quick!" I whispered to Packrat. "Over here!" We coasted behind the dumpster and jumped off our bikes. Laying them quietly on the ground, we peeked around the square, green metal container.

Mr. Goodwin stepped out his back door, a huge black trash bag in each hand. He put them down to open his bear-proof can. How was it that while everyone else in town was complaining that Lynn wasn't getting their trash fast enough, Mr. Goodwin's cans were always empty?

He put one bag inside, then picked up the other one before turning to look our way. Packrat and I ducked back behind the dumpster.

"I think he saw us!" I whispered.

Counting in my head, *one Mississippi, two Mississippi, three Missis sippi,* I hoped I was wrong. Carefully, I snuck another look. Not wrong. There he was, halfway across the parking lot, bag still in his hand!

I pulled back. "He's coming this way!"

I could hear his footsteps. How would we explain being here? Getting an ice cream? So why are we hiding? Think, think . . .

"Mr. Goodwin!"

I breathed a sigh of relief. *Thank you, Mary!*

"Good afternoon!"

"Everything okay?" I heard Mary's softer, quicker footsteps come to the dumpster. The lid opened and a bag fell inside.

"I thought I heard the bear back there," Mr. Goodwin said. "But I guess I was mistaken."

The dumpster lid slammed down. "I haven't seen her in two days," Mary said, her footsteps heading back toward the Post Office. "Maybe your new can has sent her on her way. Good riddance, I say."

I heard the post office door shut. Then I heard Mr. Goodwin drop his bag in his can and go inside.

"We've got to do this fast!" I told Packrat.

"We're only testing one this time, right?" When I nodded, he asked, "Mainely Trash or Charlie and Lynn?"

"Mainely Trash."

With our backs against the dumpster, the two of us slid around to the front. I kept lookout, while Packrat lifted the lid and dropped in the ball. Then the bat.

A low, throaty rumbling like the sound of a lawn mower came from behind us. I looked around wildly to see the bear, standing on her hind legs just behind the dumpster. How had she snuck up on us? She rumbled again, then dropped down to all fours to huff and puff our way. Even though she was a little smaller than the male at the trash dump, she still stood a good head taller than us.

"Umm—I don't have any noisemakers. I gave Mr. Goodwin my air horn." Packrat patted his pockets. "Make a run for our bikes?"

"That bear's kinda between us and our ride home!" We backed up a little. The bear came forward, walking down the side of the dumpster. We backed up a little more.

"Run?" Packrat suggested.

"Can you outrun thirty miles an hour?" I opened the dumpster lid and started to climb in. "Quick!" I urged.

"What—in there?" Packrat wrinkled his nose.

The bear took few more steps toward us.

Packrat scrambled in. "Last one in is bear food!"

I threw one leg up and rolled over the edge, sliding down the slanted front wall. I fell to my knees when I hit the trash.

I stood, stumbled, and fell again. Right away, I noticed two things: One, the dumpster didn't have one horrible smell; it had layer upon layer of them! Sweet, rotting, locker-room, musty, sour—all levels of grossness! And two, my sneakers were filling up with squishy, squashy, sticky, I-didn't-even-want-to-know-what stuff.

It was my trash nightmare come to life!

I looked around. Packrat was pinching his nose and looking in disgust at his knees, which had squished brown banana peels sticking to them.

The lid above us rattled and lifted a few inches before falling shut. It lifted again, and a hairy paw with long tan claws gripped the edge.

We backed up.

"I . . . can't . . . breathe!" Packrat gasped. He sucked in a gulp of air and held it.

Hearing more snuffling right outside, I looked around wildly for something, anything. The bat! I grabbed it, and waited. When the cover jiggled higher and a second bear paw appeared, I hit the side of the dumpster with the bat. The paw retreated. We heard the clacking of her jaws, and the paw was back. Then a nose, and a set of brown eyes. I hit the side of the dumpster again. The nose disappeared. Then reappeared, sniffing and snuffling. The lid lifted higher and I saw a bear shoulder so close, I could have reached out to pat it! If I'd wanted to lose a hand, that is.

I held up the bat, ready to poke it. "Back off!" I warned.

The shoulder and nose moved away. Then the paws pulled out. The cover slammed down.

"Guess you told her," Packrat said, with a snort.

We held our breath. Okay, from the stink, but also so we could hear what was happening outside. I put my finger to my lips. For a second I wanted to cheer. We'd done it! We'd outsmarted the bear! My heartbeat started to slow, my eyes adjusted to the darkness.

"Whew!" I said, flashing Packrat a smile. I half-waded, half-crawled to the lid. "Let's get out of here. I have no idea how I'm gonna explain to Mom why we smell—"

A roar of a different kind filled our ears. A truck?

Wait! A big truck! I listened carefully as it rolled toward us. Then it stopped. Whew! It was only parking. But then I heard a whining sound. As if a part of it was moving.

I moved to lift the lid, to show the driver that we were inside. But at that moment, the trash below us shifted and I fell left, then right. And then I felt kind of weightless, like . . . like we were being lifted in the air!

"Wait!" I called to whoever was out there. I put a hand out on the wall to steady myself, and pulled it right off when I felt something slimy. Not hearing an answer, I turned to Packrat and hollered, "Make some noise!"

I turned to hit the wall with the bat, but the dumpster rolled forward, and I fell face-first into the sea of garbage. The bat went flying who-knows-where. Packrat fell to his knees. I got up on mine and steadied myself against the wall, not caring what was on it this time.

"Wait!" I yelled again. "We're in here!"

The dumpster stopped moving. Packrat and I gave each other double high fives.

Whoosh! In one quick move, the dumpster flipped upside down, the lid swung open, and we tumbled head over heels into a bigger container. Landing on my back on a soft, squishy bag, I stared up at the upside-down dumpster we'd just left. It shook up and down, before getting pulled back out of sight, the whining sound of the forklift ringing in our ears.

Didn't anyone see us fall in?

"They can't hear us over the truck!" Packrat yelled. We heard the dumpster being set back on the ground with a crash. I stood up slowly, checking to make sure I hadn't hurt myself in the fall. My friend had spaghetti hanging from his head, and something green dripping down his vest. But we weren't laughing this time.

Cooper and Packrat: Mystery of the Bear Cub

We were stuck inside a garbage truck hopper—in Stu's Mainely Trash truck, which had come to empty the post office's dumpster. The motor of the truck revved as it backed up and away from the dumpster, beeping the whole time.

When the warning beeps stopped, the truck roared forward. I stared up at the sky and watched the tops of trees whizzing by us. "We have to show ourselves to the driver," I yelled. "Someone!"

Packrat got down on one knee and held out his locked hands. I put a foot in them and looked around for a handhold. I bounced as I said, "One, two—"

But we never got the chance to try. The trash slowly started moving, taking us with it like a wave pushes you into the shore. Only here, in the hopper, it was pushing us away from the front, where the top was open, into the rear of the hopper, which was enclosed and dark. I stumbled once, twice, as I tried to keep up with the movement. "It's compacting!" Packrat called.

A big bag hit my knees and I went down. I stared at the wall of trash rolling toward me. Closer and closer, until I was practically crossing my eyes to see it. Then it stopped. The blade that had been moving it all backward retreated to the front of the truck. I sat back to catch my breath, then stood on shaky legs.

I tried to imagine where the truck was headed, where its next stop would be. But trapped inside this container, I had no sense of direction.

The truck turned a sharp corner and slowed. Then it stopped. We tried to yell, but again, no one answered. We heard the whining sound again. Oh, no!

"Get to the sides!" I yelled. But moving through the trash was like moving through sludge. Just as we reached the slimy, ooze-covered wall, a dumpster appeared over the opening in the hopper roof. It flipped and a rain of bags fell down.

The truck took off again.

"We're going to be buried alive!" Packrat whispered. "And no one will know."

I thought about the bat Roy had used to fight off the bear. It was nowhere to be seen. Packrat might be right. I wondered how long it would take for our families to even look for us.

"Phones!" I yelled. Packrat and I tried to keep our balance as we dug into our pockets and pulled out our phones. I hit my campground contact button. The phone rang once. "Pick up! Pick up!" I cried.

The truck took a sharp left. Packrat went flying backward. Sitting up, he started looking around wildly. "My phone! I dropped it! Where'd it go?"

"Wilder Family Campground," said Mom's voice.

"Mom! Mom! We're—"

"We've stepped out of the office, and will be back in an hour. Please leave your name and number after the beep."

"Noooo!" I cried. What were the odds?

My legs were wobbly. My eyes burned. I didn't know how much more of this I could take.

"Roy! Call Roy!" Packrat urged.

Yes! I hit his contact button, and heard the phone ring. And ring. And ring. And it dawned on me.

He was still mad at me. He wasn't going to pick up.

Suddenly, the truck stopped short, tires squealing. I was thrown backward. My phone flew from my hand, smacked into the back wall, and then fell into the trash.

Packrat and I just stared after it. The universe was not on our side.

We heard yelling between two people, and then the truck rolled forward again, gears grinding.

"Umm, where exactly do garbage trucks go when their route is done?" Packrat asked.

"To the incinerator," I whispered.

We started yelling again. But after ten more minutes, we could barely talk.

When the truck shifted into a lower gear, Packrat and I looked fearfully at each other. It seemed to turn a corner, and slow to a crawl. The ground beneath got bumpier and the truck rolled from side to side before coming to a stop.

Were we about to be fried?

Chapter 27

Black bears have hearing that is twice as good as that of humans.

Beep, beep, beep. The garbage truck started backing up.

Packrat and I looked at each other. From the top of his head to the tip of his big toe, my friend was now covered in red, yellow, and green stains, like he'd fallen into a condiment factory. I had something sticky from my hip to my ankle, and paper plates, napkins, and someone's handwritten love note were stuck to me. Who knew the post office would have such disgusting trash? We smelled like rotten cheese.

What next? Was Stu picking up another dumpster? Or were we going to be dumped in the incinerator? If it was the incinerator, did they put the trash on a conveyor belt or something first, so they could look at it? Make sure there weren't any people in it?

Ha! Why would they? What normal kid crawls in a dumpster, gets tossed from that to a garbage truck, and then gets driven around town with trash raining down on them? That only happens in the movies, right?

The garbage truck engine still made a low, rumbling sound, but didn't move. I listened as well as I could above the sound. One minute turned into two. And then five.

"Maybe the driver's waiting in a line?" Packrat suggested.

"Let's try yelling again." I opened my mouth, but just then, he grabbed my arm.

"*Shhhh.*"

It was faint, but I heard the *pop-pop-pop* of tires on dirt. Another vehicle had rolled up next to us! A smaller one, from the sound of it. A door slammed. Voices. Two people talking? I couldn't quite make out what they were saying; then we heard, "Do it quick. I don't like doing this in the middle of the day."

Suddenly, Packrat and I were lifted up. The sea of trash under our feet slid toward the opening at the back.

"Climb!" I cried. Hand over hand, I tried to stay on top of the trash, Packrat right beside me.

"Look out!" Packrat yelled.

The bags of trash made my feet heavy. My foot slipped in slime. I heard Packrat grunt from the effort. The truck shifted, and I went down face-first into unbagged garbage. *Aaarrrgh!* The smell! I tried to scramble up, but was sliding down, down, down with the rest of the trash.

Suddenly, blinding sunlight hurt my eyes right before tons of trash bags landed on and around me. I lay still for a second, dazed. I wasn't sure what an incinerator looked like, but I was pretty sure this wasn't it. I started to scramble out from under the bags. Packrat hissed, "Stay still!"

I stopped to listen, peeking through the bags of trash laying on me. We were outside. In a field.

My field.

The trash dump! Mainely Trash *was* the dumper!

"I thought that car was following us at first," a familiar voice said.

"No one has any idea," another replied. "You worry too much!"

"You aren't careful enough!" the first voice barked. "If it got out that I planned this whole recycling mess so you'd get more customers and we'd pocket the extra money, they'd fire me as town manager. You'd lose all those clients I worked so hard to get for you. And your precious new truck."

Mr. Talbot.

"We can't do this forever," he continued. "This was supposed to be a quick scam. You're going to have to start bringing it all to the incinerator."

Stu's voice came from just out of my line of sight. "But they charge so much. I just need a little more money for one more truck. Then I'll be able to handle all the business you throw my way. Tell you what, let me dump here just a few more days and I'll give you a ten percent increase in your cut of the money. And I promise, I won't tell anyone you rushed the town meeting and changed the time so fewer businesspeople would be there."

Packrat was making weird little noises. I looked over, wondering if he was having trouble breathing or something, with all the trash on top of us. His eyes watered. His nose twitched.

He sneezed.

I cringed, and then heard, "Wait!"

I looked through a peephole between the bags. Talbot had a hand up. "What was that noise?"

I didn't dare breathe. Talbot took a step closer to my pile. And another. Then I heard it too, snuffling and pawing at the ground. Talbot hadn't heard Packrat—he'd heard the bear! But which bear? The big male? Or little Red? Talbot wasn't running away. In fact, he had a scowl on his face.

The sniffing got louder and louder. Something wet and cold brushed at my bare skin, just above the ankle, where the bottom of my pants had ridden up. Something sharp pawed around my sneaker, pulling the trash away from my leg.

"That cub's still here?" Talbot pointed a finger at it.

He knows about the cub? Why isn't he surprised? Wait . . .

"You're lucky the warden hasn't put two and two together!"

Stu harrumphed. "How would she ever—"

"Because, dummy, there ain't that many bear cubs with red coloring! It's a dead giveaway. Every one of those shopkeepers saw it with its mom in town. They know its color."

I gasped. Red was the cub from the back of Mr. Goodwin's store? But how? And then it dawned on me. It must have gotten here the same way we had. No wonder no one in town had seen it recently!

Packrat nudged me and mouthed the word *Jerks*.

You got that right, I mouthed back. The fact that they would leave the cub here to fend for itself, miles from its mother, made me madder than them dumping the trash.

Heavy footsteps came closer. Closer still. The snuffling stopped. Then I felt, rather than saw, the cub start to run, heavy footsteps right behind it.

"Got it!"

I heard whining. Twisting a little, I could now see Talbot holding the cub with his arms under its front legs. The cub struggled, but it couldn't go anywhere. "We'll throw it back in the truck. Take it a hundred miles from here—"

"NO!" I didn't think first. I pushed away all the trash around me and jumped from the pile. "It needs its mother!"

"It'll die without her," Packrat said, coming out right behind me.

Talbot's eyes were wide with surprise. Then they narrowed. "You."

"Me," I replied.

"You were hiding, waiting for us, under the trash?" he asked. "Clever."

"Wish I'd thought of that," I said. "Would have been a lot easier."

"Your truck brought us here," Packrat said, picking corn off his vest.

"You rode in the truck?" Stu tucked his thumbs behind his red suspenders and pulled them out, then brought them back in as he gave a big belly laugh. "How'd that work out for you?"

"My idiot cousin!" Talbot snapped. "How did you not notice two kids fall from the dumpster into your truck?" He shook his head. In a quieter, scarier voice, he said, "I'm done playing. We've got to get out of here. Quick. Take this cub, Stu."

"No!" I kicked Talbot in the knee.

"Ow!" Dropping Red, Talbot grabbed his foot and started hopping around, as Stu lunged for me. I ducked from his hand.

"Back off!" Packrat threw a rotten tomato, hitting Stu square in the face. He stopped to wipe his eyes, but Packrat just pelted him with another one. He turned to make a grab for Packrat, and tripped, landing face-first in something that looked like lime-green slime. Only I don't think that's what it was.

"Ewww!" Packrat and I cried, as he sat up. All we could see were his eyes.

I looked around wildly as Stu tried to wipe his face off. "Where's the cub?"

"There!" Packrat pointed. The back end of the cub was disappearing into the woods. It was safe!

But we weren't. Not yet.

Talbot charged at us.

"Run!" Packrat yelled. "The woods!"

I didn't have to be told twice.

Chapter 28

Adult black bears are at the top of the food chain. Their only predators are grizzlies, other black bears, and humans.

I was never so glad to see the cover of trees and bushes.

I scanned for the cub, running as fast as my feet could carry me. I heard the pounding footsteps of Packrat on my right.

Behind us, Talbot was screaming at Stu, telling him we were getting away.

I leapt over a log and kept running. There was only one place I could think of to hide.

Leading Packrat, I ran to the dig site and over to some bushes by the privy hole. The shovels were right where we'd left them.

"One for you, one for me," I told him.

"Now what?" Packrat asked between breaths. His chest rose and fell with each one. "Head for the water?"

I shook my head. "I bet they'll think we followed the trail. Let's hide here till they leave."

Packrat pointed to the camouflaged privy hole. "In there?"

Hearing the crashing and swearing of the two men as they raced through the woods, I winced.

"No time to tie the rope and climb down." I pointed. "Fireplace."

We rushed over to it and ducked inside. Standing up, my face suddenly felt as if a thousand tiny threads brushed across it. Spiderwebs! Rubbing my free hand all over my face, I shuddered.

It was darker here, in the firebox, but there was still enough light to see. The flue was bigger than I'd thought. Big enough so Packrat and I could both stand. Backing up as far as we could into the sides, we listened. And waited.

Hearing a small cry, I stilled. Whining. Panting.

I really didn't want to leave my hiding spot, but the sound was so pitiful. I crouched down to peek out, and there, half in and half out of the old well, was Red. The cub must have fallen in, in its hurry to get away from Talbot! The poor thing clawed at the earth, trying to climb out. Its mouth kept opening, but the cry that came out was weak and tired. And scared.

"Grab it and come back!" Packrat cried.

More crashing and cursing, louder now. I peeked over the wall and saw the red of Stu's suspenders weaving and bobbing through the woods. Talbot and Stu weren't on the trail; they were coming this way. Packrat pulled me back inside the shadows of the firebox.

"I can't leave Red," I whispered.

"You can't help the cub at all, if you get caught!"

Packrat had a point. I didn't want to leave the little bear, but maybe it could hold on for a few more minutes. We tucked ourselves inside the flue again. From here, I couldn't see the cub, but I could hear its faint cries. At least I could until the loudmouths, Talbot and Stu, arrived.

Their footsteps slowed to tromps on the other side of the wall. I hoped they would fall into our privy hole. They paced. They seemed to be going away, then one set of footsteps stopped.

"What's that?" Talbot said.

"I didn't hear anything," Stu grumbled. "Those nosy kids are gone. We'll never find them out here!" He swore, and I thought I heard him kick a tree or something.

"Oh, settle down, would you?" Talbot said.

"You know as well as I do that when they get back to that camp-ground, they're going to say they saw us!" Stu was whining now. "No one will want to hire me, once the town knows. If I don't make money, I don't keep the truck—"

"You'll keep your truck. I just had a great idea. I'm going to get rid of your competition."

Packrat and I shared a look. *Lynn?*

"I'm going to tell everyone we caught that woman and her kid dumping trash here."

"But the brats saw us here!"

Talbot chuckled. "They saw concerned citizens trying to help. We found a bag of Goodwin's trash; in fact, I've got it in my car. I heard he hired Lynn—"

The cub whined, louder this time. I could hear its paws scratching in the dirt and rocks that I knew circled the well.

"Hear that? The kids are hiding here and they're crying!" Stu laughed. "The big babies! Not so tough now!"

Packrat stirred, and I held out my arm to stop him. Good thing Roy wasn't here. Being called a baby would have been something he couldn't have ignored. He'd have gone out there, fists flying, insults hurled.

"Don't be stupid," we heard Talbot say. His footsteps came closer to the end of the wall. "It's not the kids. Look! It's the cub! Well, well, well. Looks like nature's going to take care of that piece of evidence for us."

We heard the cub whine, and more dirt plopped into the water inside the well. Red must be tearing up the sides! Talbot laughed. "That cub will look like it fell in and drowned. An accident."

They weren't going to help it? What the heck? I ducked to step out of our hiding spot but Packrat grabbed hold of my shirt and hauled me back. When he did, my hand grabbed the wall and pulled a rock from it. It fell to the solid firebox floor.

CRAAAAAACK!

The whole forest went quiet. Even the cub.

"You hear that?" Stu whispered.

"Shut up and listen!" A minute later we heard, "You go that way. I'll take this side."

I looked at Packrat. This was it; our cover was blown. They'd be looking in every nook and cranny now that I had given us away.

Their footsteps got closer. And closer still. But just as their shoe tips came into view, a stick broke up on the hill, by the stairs that led nowhere. And then another broke down by the bottle dump.

Stu laughed. "Looks like we're chasing ghosts. Why would they hide? They're long gone, running home to tell their parents."

We heard their footsteps moving away from the cellar hole, back toward the trail.

"C'mon," Talbot said. "We've got some trouble to cause."

Chapter 29

Less than half the cubs born in a year will make it to their first birthday. Starvation is the biggest cause of death.

I hadn't heard Red for a few minutes. Had the cub gotten too tired to hang on? Or had it gotten out?

We listened to the footsteps of Talbot and Stu fade until we couldn't hear them anymore, then bolted from our hiding place to race for Red. When we were four feet away, I put out an arm to stop Packrat from running all the way. I could see how the frantic digging of the cub with its claws had weakened the sides of the old well. I was afraid our weight would collapse it and hurt Red.

Looking around, I picked up a small but long log. Sliding it over, next to the cub's paws, I urged him, "Grab on!" But I didn't count on the little guy being so exhausted. The cub didn't even try to grab hold. He actually shrank back, eyes wide and scared. I guess I would too, if someone put a log in my face.

"Okay, boy." I pulled the log back. New plan. Getting down on my stomach, to spread out my weight like a snowshoe would, I kept my eyes on the cub and told Packrat to hold my feet. Once I felt his hands on my ankles, I elbow-crawled slowly over to Red. All the way, I tried not to think about the damage those sharp claws could do to me. When I reached the edge of the well, I put my hands in the cold water to grab the cub just below its front legs. It struggled to turn away from me, waving its paws and splashing me. I tried to talk to it like I'd talk to Molly if she'd fallen and hurt herself, but still it fought me. The more it wiggled, the more the wall broke apart.

Maybe I should pull back, I thought.

Suddenly, from over my head, a piece of green cloth fell to cover the bear's head. He went still.

Packrat's vest! But, if Packrat's hands were on my ankles, then how did the vest . . . Feeling the bear squirm, I shook my head. Rescue first.

Pulling with everything I had, Red and the vest slid out of the hole, all in one bundle. The cub shivered. I didn't know if it was from fear or from the fact that it was soaking wet from shoulders to tail. I rolled the vest off its head, keeping the rest of its body tight inside it.

I swear the cub closed its eyes in relief.

Under me, the well wall crumbled some more, rocks plopping into the water. I wrapped my arms around the bundle of bear cub.

"Pull me back!" The hands on my feet tugged me back over the forest floor. When I was far enough from the well, I rolled over and sat up, bundle and all.

And there was Roy, rubbing his hands together, Packrat and Charlie crouching with him. I just sat there, my mouth hanging open so wide a frog could have jumped inside.

"They heard everything!" Packrat said. "They're the ones who made all the noises in the woods, breaking sticks and stuff, so Talbot and Stu didn't look for us," Packrat added, with a goofy, our-best-friend-is-back grin.

The cub squirmed a bit. Packrat came over to take him while I stood up.

"But how did you know?" I asked.

Roy put his hands in his pockets. "When I calmed down, you know? I biked into town to catch up with you, and saw the garbage truck pulling out of the back of the post office. I looked all over, but I only found your bikes. I looked in Mr. Goodwin's but you weren't there either. So I called your mom just to see if you'd come back, which was a mistake, because when she found out I wasn't with you, she asked a gazillion questions."

One side of his mouth went up in a half-smile.

"She is good! I tried not to tell her anything, but she figured out what I didn't say. How does she do that?"

As Roy told his story, we started walking, fast, toward the field. I wasn't going to let those guys get away if I could help it.

"So I guess your mom got worried and decided to drive around town and look for you," Roy continued. "By the time I biked back to the campground, the store was closed and all the adults were out looking. But Charlie was there on the porch, and we put two and two together."

"What did you think we'd done?" Packrat passed Red back to me. The cub was heavier than it looked, like carrying four, or maybe five, of those five-pound bags of sugar.

"Charlie and I decided you'd seen the garbage truck and decided to climb on the back and hitch a ride to see where they were dumping. Which was here, so we canoed over to find you."

"Well, we hitched a ride all right," Packrat said, slapping Roy on the back. "Oh, boy. You missed a great adventure."

"We didn't ride on the back of the truck," I added. "We rode *in* it."

Roy thought about that for a minute. He looked us up and down, taking in our filthy, stained, stinky clothes. "You mean, the *back,* back?"

Packrat and I nodded.

"No wonder you two smell so bad! How'd you get in there?"

"Dumpster!" Packrat and I said at the same time.

Roy whistled low, as he held a branch back for Charlie to pass. "Now *that* must have been something."

"You guys do this all the time?" Charlie was breathing hard from trying to keep up with us. "Cool!"

I had to admit, the kid was doing great.

"How's the cub?" Roy asked.

"Stressed." I looked down at it. "And probably dehydrated, too. But now we know where its mother is, and once it's back with her, it should get better."

Charlie looked into the woods around us fearfully. "The mother? Is she here?"

"No, she's back in town," I reassured him. We had reached the wall and crouched down behind it.

"How'd Red get—" Roy's eyebrows went up. "Let me guess; same way you did."

Looking across the field, I breathed a sigh of relief. Stu and Talbot were still there, talking by the garbage truck. I pointed at them.

"They're the reason that mother bear is behind the store so much! Sure, she was looking for food, but she was also looking for her cub. I bet she thinks it's still in that dumpster."

"You wouldn't have all this extra business if it wasn't for me!" Talbot's voice carried down the field, making us all look his way. "Whose idea was it to use that dumb kid's project as an excuse to close the transfer station for a couple of weeks, huh?" He pointed at Stu. "So remember that! We're going to do this my way."

I had no idea what they were arguing about now, and I didn't care. I just needed them to stay put, until the adults got here. I knew they'd figure it out.

I just hoped it wouldn't take too long.

"Cooper?" Charlie put a hand on my arm. "You aren't going to let him blame my mom for this trash, are you? I like it here. I even like the job." He ducked his head. "Well, kinda."

"Don't worry," I told him. "They aren't leaving this field if we can help it. But you have to do something for me." I handed the bear bundle to Charlie, who was kneeling on the ground next to a big oak tree. "Watch the cub; we call it Red. Keep it wrapped up," I instructed, although I didn't need to. The cub was still exhausted and not moving much. "I want to deliver it to Warden Kate, so she can check it out." Taking off my sweatshirt, I laid it over the vest. "If it struggles, cover its head again."

"You're going out there?" Charlie's eyes got wide. "With those two bad guys?"

I nodded.

"So what's the plan?" Packrat had the binoculars and was scoping out the field.

I shook my head. For once, I didn't have a plan.

Chapter 30

A hibernating bear's heart rate slows from its usual forty to fifty beats per minute down to eight, and it takes one breath every forty-five seconds.

"What have we got to work with?" I asked, scanning the field. *Think, think, think.* We had to keep these two guys here for a little longer. "Two cars, mounds of trash, a shovel." I looked to Packrat hopefully.

Opening his vest, he pulled out a hunk of rope, a garden trowel, a walkie-talkie, and a screwdriver.

"Sorry, guys. I had no time to plan for hiding in a dumpster," said Packrat, "and being hauled here in the back of a garbage truck. Even if I'd known, how do you pack for that?"

Garbage truck. My gaze went to Stu's shiny, brand-new, electric blue garbage truck.

Roy's eyes lit up. "I've always wanted to see the inside of one of those!" But then he frowned. "But not in the back. Never in the hopper! You guys stink!"

"Okay. We're going to wing it. Whatever happens, stay here!" I told Charlie again. His eyes were wide with fright. I didn't think he'd be going anywhere.

Packrat lowered his binoculars and pointed right, to the far edge of the field. "We got trouble."

I grinned. "Uh-uh. Looks more like Talbot and Stu have trouble."

Just emerging from the woods was the big male bear. Sniffing the air, he didn't look too happy to see these guys hanging around his private dining room.

Stu and Talbot hadn't seen the bear yet; their backs were to him. But boy, it was going to be a great show when they did!

Talbot opened his driver-side door and leaned inside. *No, no, no,* I thought. *Don't leave now!* But instead, he pulled out a big, square map that was all folded up. Leaving his door open, he walked back to spread the map out on the hood. Stu went to stand beside him.

Here was our chance!

Bent over, I jogged to the first mound. Peeking over it, I saw the men's heads, still bent over the map.

I waved my friends forward. Keeping low, I moved to the next pile. This mound was taller, so keeping my back to it, I slid around to peek from the side. Talbot looked up from the map to talk to Stu.

I held up my hand so my friends would stay at the first mound. When the men went back to the map, I moved fast, but silently, to the truck. Reaching the side of it, I stood up against it, trying to catch my breath. The adults were out of my line of sight now.

I opened the passenger-side door as quietly as I could and climbed up, so I could see out the windshield. Talbot's car was parked, pointing at the truck, only about a hundred feet away. The bear was still plodding across the field, moving slowly, stalking the men.

Talbot pointed at a spot on the map. "So you know where that is? Are you happy now? Keep dumping for one more week, and yes, I'll take that extra share of the money you've been making. But then you have to stop! Someone will figure it out in time. They find you, they find me."

I waved my friends forward. They got to the second pile.

Talbot stood and started folding the map.

I held up my hand for my friends to hold. How were they going to get over to me without him—?

Suddenly, a breeze lifted the map out of his hands, and it floated to the ground. When the men bent to retrieve it, it floated away toward the open field.

"Get that map!" Talbot yelled.

This was our chance! I waved my friends to the truck. They bolted—and made it!

Or, Packrat did. Roy kept going, sliding down the side of the garbage truck toward the back end.

"Roy!" I hissed. "Stop!" He just grinned at me, before sliding around the corner, out of sight.

"Bear!" Stu's voice brought my gaze back to them. "It's a big one!"

"Don't yell, you idiot!" Talbot yelled.

I shook my head.

Stu shoved Talbot. "*You're* yelling!"

I don't know if it was all the angry voices, or if he just wanted to see what was going on, but the bear got up on his hind legs and shook his head.

I crawled over all the buttons and levers and shifts to get over to the driver's side, so Packrat could climb into the passenger seat. In the rearview mirror, I saw Roy make a dash from the back of the garbage truck to the back of Talbot's car.

"Don't run!" Talbot said. "The warden said they're more afraid of you than you are of them!"

The bear dropped down on all fours. He stared at the men, then suddenly, very quickly, took a one-step, rolling hop in their direction like he was going to run at them. Both men jumped backwards, falling for the bear's bluff.

"Who's afraid of wh-wh-who?" Stu was shaking in his boots.

Talbot pulled on Stu's arm, urging him backward, toward the car. I tried to signal Roy to get back here, but he was already at Talbot's open driver-side door. Crouched down behind it, he hit the lock button and slowly shut the door.

And there stood Talbot. Stu ran to the car door and pulled on the handle, trying frantically to open it.

"Where the heck did you come from?" Talbot grabbed my friend's arm, hauling him up on his feet. "And you locked the car? Are you crazy?"

"You're not going anywhere now." Roy lifted his chin. "And you aren't pinning this mess on Lynn."

Packrat and I exchanged worried glances. The bear was on all fours now, slowly stalking Talbot.

"Don't look now," Roy said, pointing behind the big man. "The bear's coming for you."

Talbot turned, and started walking backward around the trunk of the car, dragging Roy with him. Stu followed behind them.

"If we get eaten, you get eaten . . ." I heard Talbot say.

Talbot thrust Roy at Stu. "Keep hold of him," he barked.

As the bear rounded the back of the car, all three of them started backing up.

Seeing the truck key on the dash, I put it in the ignition. "Maybe if I start this thing, it'll distract them long enough to let go of Roy."

Packrat threw a hand out toward all the knobs and levers between us and along the dash. "I'll see if I can figure out what some of these controls can do."

The bear, the men, and Roy were all in front of the truck now. Turning the key, I felt—and heard—the truck roar to life. The bear froze for a second, and so did Talbot and Stu, who had a tight hold of Roy's arm.

This didn't work out quite the way I'd hoped.

Talbot slowly turned, and, shading his eyes, looked through the windshield.

"Who's in there?" he demanded. Seeing Packrat and me, he glared at Roy. "I shoulda known you weren't here alone!"

"Get out of my truck!" Stu bellowed.

"A better idea would be to open up and let us in!" Talbot tipped his head toward Roy. "Or I'll tell Stu to feed your friend to the bear first."

"Don't you dare!" Roy said to me. "You had your fun; now let me have mine." He must have seen the hesitation in my face, because he added, "You let them in, and we're all trapped! Trust me, I got this!"

Well, maybe he *did* have this, but that didn't mean Packrat and I couldn't help.

The bear shook its head, blowing and huffing, reminding the men it was still there. Without warning, it raced forward, charging them. They all froze, standing stiff like boards, Stu closing his eyes and pulling Roy in front of him like a shield. But the bear stopped short, just inches from their feet. Backing up, it huffed.

"C'mon, let Roy go," I muttered. I really thought Stu would, right then, when the bear bluff-charged them.

"I don't like this." Packrat was flipping levers like crazy. "That bear's gonna eat them!"

The wipers went on. Lights began to blink. We even felt the hopper wall slide forward, like it would to squish the trash.

"As long as they don't do anything stupid, the bear shouldn't attack."

At least, I didn't think it would. Trash-dump bears didn't act normally. But then again, this dump hadn't been there for very long. I held my hand over the horn, just in case. The thing was, Roy was right. If I scared the bear off now, these guys might overpower us, take back the vehicles, and make it out of there.

The light went on in the cab. The hopper started to lift, to dump.

Both men and Roy stood stone-still through it all, Stu cowering behind Roy. The bear was still staring them down. Finally, it huffed again, pawed the ground. Then it turned to go.

Roy started pulling, trying to break free from Stu.

Talbot laughed at the retreating bear. "See! Stand your ground, and they back off."

The bear paused to look back and huff again. Talbot squared his shoulders. Picking up a rotten orange from the ground, he threw it at the bear, hitting its back paw. "Yeah! Get out of here!" He grabbed another one and threw that, too, missing this time.

"What are you doing?" Stu yelled. He started backing up, dragging Roy with him.

"Stop it, you jerk!" Roy said, trying again to break away from Stu. I could see he wanted to tackle Talbot to the ground.

Talbot threw a third orange, this time hitting the bear on the rump. "We gotta make sure it goes away!"

The black bear turned back, eyes narrowed. I imagined it saying, *You really wanna go another round with me?*

Suddenly, the forks, which were meant to pick up dumpsters, inched upward to waist height. The bear had taken a step forward, so the men didn't notice.

But Roy did.

His eyes went from the fork arms to Packrat and me. I pointed to Stu and the big red X the suspenders made on his back. And in an instant, all three of us knew how to take him out.

Talbot bent to pick up another orange, just as the bear bluff-charged again. When he turned, still bent at the waist, he found himself nose to nose with the big black bear.

Stu backed up toward the truck, distancing himself from the bear-versus-man standoff.

Roy nudged him a little to the left, putting the right fork arm in a perfect line with the X on his back. In one move, with his free hand, Roy lifted the suspenders and dropped them onto the fork. Packrat flipped the lever, and the arm lifted, taking Stu with it.

"One down!" I cheered.

"One to go!" shouted Roy.

Chapter 31

*Newborn black bear cubs, born during hibernation,
are totally dependent on their mother. They weigh less
than a pound, have very little fur, and can barely crawl.*

When the fork arm jerked Stu up onto his toes, he let Roy go.
When it lifted him off his feet, he started grabbing for my friend again,
trying to stay on the ground with him. But Roy fought him off easily,
and looked up, laughing, as Packrat used the lever to raise Stu higher
and higher.

"Put me down! Put me down!" he cried, legs and arms waving,
trying to connect with anything solid.

But there was nothing solid he could find at seven feet off the
ground.

Even the bear and Talbot were staring up. Yelling and cursing, Stu
made quite a sight as he swayed back and forth, while trying to get his
arms behind his back to lift the suspenders off the fork arm.

The bear huffed and took a step back. Getting up on its hind legs,
it sniffed the air. I imagined it was wondering what kind of bird Stu was.
The bear plopped down on all four paws, got a little closer to Stu, and
stood again.

His nose sniffed the air just under Stu's waving feet.

"Whew!" I said. "Good thing he has heavy-duty suspenders on.
Just two inches lower and—"

Stu's left suspender slipped off its button and he dropped a couple
of inches, then stopped, before swinging side to side. The second suspender was stretched to the limit, but it held. Barely . . .

The bear sniffed his boots.

Seeing Talbot backing away, Stu cried, "D-d-d-do something! Don't
leave me here!"

Talbot paused. He looked at the bear, and then at the orange he was still gripping in his right hand.

"He wouldn't!" I rolled down my window, as Roy ran over to jump on the running board.

"Talbot," I yelled, "don't do it! Everybody just stand still!"

Either he didn't hear me over Stu, who was calling his name, or he was too stupid to care. He threw the orange at the bear, hitting him smack in the back of the head.

The bear dropped to all fours faster than I'd ever seen before. It turned and charged Talbot without warning.

And this time, it was no bluff.

It didn't stop.

Talbot ran backwards for half a second, before he turned and ran as fast as he could go, into the woods, the bear chasing after him. Pack-rat and I scrambled out of the truck.

Roy looked up at Stu, who was once again trying to reach behind himself to unhook the last suspender.

"I wouldn't do that if I were you," he said. "Without the suspenders, you're going down."

When Stu kept at it, Roy started walking backwards. "You fall, break a leg, and the bear comes back, we aren't going to be here to save you."

Stu went still. "What? Where are you going? Don't leave me up here!" But he'd stopped moving.

The three of us turned and ran after the bear and Talbot. If the bear wanted to catch him, he would. And I wouldn't have blamed the bear, after what Talbot had done to provoke him. But I suspected the bear only wanted to chase Talbot off what he now considered to be his territory. I just hoped he wouldn't give up the chase too easily. We still had to trap Talbot so he couldn't leave.

And I finally had a plan.

Racing after Talbot, my friends and I passed Charlie, who was still in his hiding spot with the cub. He stood up to come with us, but I waved him back down.

"Stay there!" I told him. "Watch Red."

Praying Talbot was headed for the only place he knew around here—the old cellar hole and well, where he'd abandoned Red—we circled wide around it so we could sneak up behind him. Stepping quietly through the cellar wall opening, we took in the situation.

Talbot was backing up in our direction, away from the bear, which was clacking its jaws and blowing at him. I knew, any minute, it would bluff-charge again.

In fact, I was counting on it.

Positioning ourselves right behind the privy hole with the camouflage cover, I whisper-called, "Talbot! *Psst!* Talbot!"

He looked at us. His scowl was gone, replaced by fear.

"This way!" Packrat urged. When Talbot began race-walking toward us, Packrat said, "Not too fast!"

As I watched the town manager shaking in his shoes, I felt bad tricking him like this. But he'd done some terrible tricking of his own.

Never taking his eyes off the bear, Talbot inched closer and closer to us. The bear continued to clack its jaws over and over. The sound was even making me jumpy. I backed up a step from the privy hole.

CRACK! Talbot stepped on a stick. The sound startled him, and made him stumble backward. The bear bluff-charged. Talbot turned to run at us, and stepped right on the camouflage cover. I could tell the minute he realized something wasn't right. He froze in place, staring at us, his eyes growing confused as the ground gave way beneath his feet. He made a grab for me and got a fistful of shirt, right before the cover broke under his weight, and he went down.

I was pulled to the ground. Packrat and Roy grabbed ahold of me, yanking me back. My shirt slipped from Talbot's hand, and seconds later, we heard him land with a thud on the dirt floor below.

All three of us scrambled to the edge and got on our stomachs to look down.

Roy joked, "I think we just flushed him down the privy!"

Talbot lay at the bottom, dazed and confused. Moaning, he sat up, his hand on his head. The walls were too high for him to climb out. Here he would stay until we could bring the adults back.

The three of us, still panting from the run and excitement, looked at each other and smiled.

Clack, clack, clack.

We'd forgotten about the bear.

Still lying on our stomachs, we looked across the privy hole to find the animal pawing the ground and blowing at us.

"Slowly get up," I said quietly. I got on my knees, then to my feet, my arms wide, my eyes on the bear.

I hadn't thought of anything beyond catching Talbot. Maybe somewhere in the back of my mind, I thought the bear would just huff and storm off.

Instead, he turned his anger on us.

The three of us slowly walked backward away from the privy, as the bear circled around it. I found it kind of cruelly ironic: We were in the same situation Talbot had been in.

Packrat patted his pockets. "I've got nothing to make noise with!"

Then, suddenly, there was nowhere to go. We were up against the cellar hole wall. The bear snorted, stopped. He got up on his hind legs and shook his head.

"We aren't the enemy," I whispered. Putting a hand up, I added, "We aren't gonna hurt you."

He dropped to all fours before making that low, throaty, rumbling sound. The three of us stood shoulder to shoulder, facing it.

"It's gonna bluff-charge again," I warned my friends. "Don't move! Look away!"

In a flash, the bear took three running steps toward us, stopping short. My heart was racing so fast, I could hear my pulse in my head. My legs shook so bad, I wasn't sure how I was still standing. I cast my eyes down and away toward the fireplace, trying to show the bear we meant him no harm.

The bear huffed once, twice. He backed up two steps, and then huffed again.

Then, turning completely, he raced off into the woods.

All three of us slid down the wall into a heap.

"That was sooo cooool!" Packrat said between heavy breaths. "But let's not ever do it again."

Chapter 32

Black bears mark their territory by biting, clawing, and rubbing their scent on trees near their trail. These are called marking trees.

Right after the bear left, we heard Charlie and Warden Kate calling our names. This, in turn, had Talbot hollering from the privy hole.

Once we had the warden by our side, she radioed her assistant who was waiting by her truck in the field and told him to call the police. Packrat gently fished out a hunk of rope from his vest, which was still covering the cub, and we lowered it in the hole to get Talbot out. Warden Kate cuffed him and led him from the woods, as Packrat, Roy, Charlie, and I explained everything on the way.

No sooner had we stepped from the woods than my dad's truck rolled into the field. I swear Mom and Dad jumped out of the truck before it stopped rolling, and raced toward us. Seeing Warden Kate with Talbot handcuffed, and Stu hollering from up high, Dad tipped his hat back to look me in the eye.

"We're too late again, aren't we?"

"Well, I'll be—" Mom just stared at the swinging Stu, not able to finish her sentence.

The warden moved to the garbage truck to lower Stu, just as Mr. Goodwin drove into the field. Behind him came Lynn, her truck mounded high with trash. She parked and jumped out, not even bothering to close her door, and rushed over. "Charlie?"

"Here I am, Mom!" He stepped through the crowd, handing me the bundled-up cub just before his mom swept him up into a big hug. She pushed him back and, with her hands on his shoulders, looked him up and down. "Are you okay? Are you hurt? Where have you been?" She hugged him tight again.

Cooper and Packrat: Mystery of the Bear Cub

My mom caught my eye and smiled.

I walked over, and she put a finger under my chin so she could lift it and look over every inch of my face. Seeing no cuts or bruises, she looked down to the bundle in my arms.

"I suppose this little guy was in trouble?" she asked, peeling back a corner of Packrat's vest to see the cub's whole face. I knew right then and there, her heart melted.

"So these are your trash dumpers," Mr. Goodwin said, as Warden Kate lowered Stu to the ground.

I cleared my throat.

"Umm, Mr. Goodwin, I have to ask." This was the one part of the mystery we hadn't solved. "We put a baseball bat in the dumpster and it ended up back here. That's why we suspected Stu and Talbot. But we, umm . . ."

"We put a ball in your trash can—" Packrat said.

"—and it ended up here, too!" Roy finished.

I looked at Lynn and Charlie. "And since Mr. Goodwin was paying you to take away his trash—"

"Cooper!" Mom cried. "How could you accuse—"

Lynn put up a hand. "It's okay," she said to Mom. "Cooper, I don't pick up Mr. Goodwin's trash."

I stopped. "But Dad sent you over so he could sign up for your services. And he said you were there . . ."

Lynn raised an eyebrow.

"You were there talking to him," I finished. That sounded lame, even to my ears. We never actually saw her take his trash, and Mr. Goodwin had never said he'd hired her. We had just assumed.

Charlie's eyes narrowed. He was mad, and I couldn't blame him. He'd saved Oscar, and just helped us save the bear cub, and here we were, accusing him of dumping trash.

Lynn shook her head. "We asked Mr. Goodwin if he wanted us to take his trash. He said no."

"But . . ." I was still confused. "The ball?"

We all looked to the store owner.

"I was cheating." Mr. Goodwin hung his head. "I didn't want to pay for something I had gotten for free before. Not even Lynn's fees. So I snuck my trash into the post office dumpster whenever I could. Which was often. But I have never"—and he looked me straight in the eye—"never dumped my trash here. Not even so much as a scrap of paper." That explained why the post office dumpster was full of food waste!

I looked back to where the warden was bringing a handcuffed Stu over to Talbot.

A car raced onto the field, much the same way my parents' had. I looked over at Roy and I swear his eyebrows lifted off his forehead.

"Dad?" he whispered.

"There's my lawyer!" Talbot barked, seeing Mr. Parker storming over. "Now you'll have to uncuff me, Warden."

Roy looked from his dad to Talbot. "You can't let him go!"

"Get over here and tell her, Parker!" Talbot ordered, his face all blotchy red. "Get them to take the cuffs off me! Set them straight with all your lawyer stuff."

Mr. Parker walked toward Talbot. Roy jogged alongside, grabbing at his sleeve.

"Dad? C'mon. Cooper and Packrat, they were just protecting the Wilders' property. He harassed a bear! Don't—"

With Mr. Parker there, Talbot had gotten braver. He squared his shoulders and looked down on Warden Kate.

"Go on, Parker. Tell her. She can't cuff me. Dumping trash is not a prison crime! We'll pay the stupid fine and walk—"

Mr. Parker raised his arm and punched Talbot in the nose.

Now I knew who Roy took after in his family.

"Hey!" screamed Stu. "You can't do that! You're his lawyer."

"Not anymore." Mr. Parker shook his hand, but he was smiling like a bear that had just found a honeycomb.

"But . . . what happened to all that attorney–client privilege stuff?" Roy asked.

"When he tangled with you, all that went away," Mr. Parker explained. "I'm taking myself off this case because he messed with my boy." Mr. Parker hesitantly put a hand on Roy's shoulder. "Are you okay? Are you hurt anywhere? Your mother is going to kill me!"

Watching this, I remembered how many times my parents had hugged me and questioned me and oh-you-poor-thing-ed me after an adventure. Packrat's mom was a master at it, too. And every time, Roy had rolled his eyes and laughed at us. But now I knew that underneath, he was a little bit jealous of all the attention we'd gotten.

So when Packrat snickered, I knew it wasn't meant to be mean.

Roy caught my eye. I smirked in a how-do-you-like-it kind of way. And just like that, all was right with the world again.

Chapter 33

While still hibernating, a mother bear keeps her newborns warm by curling up around them, hovering and breathing on them.

"It's going to cost a lot of money and take a lot of time to clean up this trash dump," Mom said sadly, as she looked at the seven mounds and carpet of trash surrounding us.

Lynn put a hand on my mom's arm. "Charlie and I will do what we can with the cleanup. You've been so good to us, and we appreciate everything you're doing to help us get back on our feet."

"We'll help, too," Roy's dad said.

Mr. Goodwin nodded. "Be glad to!"

Dad tipped his hat back. "We're gonna have to work fast. According to Cooper, it's already attracted a lot of animals, including a big bear and this cub."

Warden Kate looked down at Red. "Does it belong to the bear you saw here?"

"Nope, this one belongs to the town bear! It's her cub! That's why she kept coming back behind Mr. Goodwin's store."

The warden shook her head and smiled. "Start again. Talk slowly."

"Stu accidentally brought the bear cub here in the garbage truck," I said.

"It must have been dumpster-diving with its mom when Stu drove up and emptied it into his truck," Packrat added. "Kinda like how we got here."

"How do you know?" Warden Kate asked.

"The cub behind the store was red," Mr. Goodwin offered.

I pointed to Talbot. "And I heard them talking about it. They knew they'd done it, when Red spilled out with the trash."

She turned to the men. "And you never told anyone? Tried to catch it? Bring it back to its mother?" With every word, her voice got higher and higher.

Talbot shrugged. With a glare from the warden, he tipped his head toward Stu.

"He tried to catch it, but it was too fast. And if we'd told you, you would've figured out who was dumping here."

"Now I have an angry mother bear in town," the warden scolded. "She isn't settling down, either. On my way here, I got another call from Mary at the post office. The mother bear has run out of chances."

"But . . ." Roy's face got panicky. "What if we bring the cub back?"

"They've got to be together," Charlie chimed in, leaning on his own mother a bit.

"I don't think we can," said the warden. "The mother has learned that by being aggressive, people will run away and she can have all the food she needs. Think about it. Would you go back to foraging if you always knew where you could find a good, tasty meal for you and your cub?"

Lynn grimaced. "I wouldn't. I'd stay put."

"I'm afraid we might have to . . . to put her down," said Warden Kate, with a sympathetic look.

"No!" I cried. "It's not her fault. It's theirs!" I pointed to Talbot and Stu.

"Oh, you're right, of course," the warden said, shaking her head back and forth. "I suppose we can try relocating them. But it may not work. Bears can travel great distances for food, and once they figure out how easy picking trash can be over picking blueberries—"

"Blueberries?" I had almost forgotten! "There are tons of blueberry bushes over by the cellar hole!" Remembering something else we'd seen there, I asked, "But will the other bear be a problem? The male one?"

She shook her head. "Not necessarily."

"But this stupid trash." Packrat threw a hand out toward the mounds. "That *is* a problem, isn't it?"

Warden Kate scowled at Talbot and Stu, who were being loaded into the back of a police car. "It's a problem for *them*. They'll be paying for the equipment needed to clean your field up for you."

"So we don't have to do it?" Roy seemed relieved. "For a minute there, I thought Mr. Wilder was going to make us work overtime to clean it up."

"I suspect that the changes have already been made, and Talbot and Stu were only keeping it closed to haul more trash, and make more money. Once the townspeople know what Talbot was up to, they'll reopen the transfer station bright and early Monday morning."

"Open for residents—but we still can't use it," Dad pointed out. "Recycling was voted in; it's happening. So we'll keep them for the rest of this summer." Dad nodded toward Lynn and Charlie, who were talking to Mom off to the side. "Besides, I like the idea of recycling. But I think the smaller businesses and the homeowners should be able to use it again. The town will need to come up with a plan that works for everybody, and not be in such a hurry to get it done."

"I, for one, say it's about time!" Mr. Goodwin's eyes twinkled. "I never could have stayed open if I'd had to pay someone to haul my trash."

"But Dad," I said, tugging on his sleeve until he looked down at me. "Will Lynn lose all her business when people can go back to the town transfer station? And when we close for the winter—where will she and Charlie live?"

Dad shook his head, and Mr. Goodwin's eyes became sad.

Even I knew there weren't enough bottles in that dump to help them.

Chapter 34

Black bears will usually make their summer beds in a cool, damp, mossy area.

The very next day, we kayaked back over with Charlie for two reasons: One, I'd woken up in the middle of the night in a panic after dreaming about woodland animals falling into the well, one after the other, only this time, there was no one there to save them. We had to go back to stuff it full of rocks from the wall, and fast.

And two, it was time to fill in the privy hole for the same reason. Especially now that the bears were coming.

Before we did, though, we wanted to dig a little deeper for one last shot at that gold. At the very least, maybe we'd find more stuff like the Maine Militia button.

My friends and I convinced Charlie's mom to let him tag along, and we gave him a turn in rotation with the jobs, too. It was the least we could do after he'd saved Oscar and the cub.

Now, after an hour of filling in the well, and two hours of digging, all we had to show for our work was another button Packrat had found at the sifter, and a creepy, ceramic doll head Roy had dug up. Not the body, just the head. With one eye staring at us. Unblinking.

"I don't know about you guys," I said, "but that's going to give me nightmares for weeks."

"Maybe we ought to quit here," Packrat suggested. "While we're ahead." He looked at us all expectantly. "Get it?" he asked. "A head?"

I rolled my eyes, and punched him in the arm. Roy groaned. But Charlie said, "Not really."

After Packrat explained it to him, I told my friends there was only time for one more shovelful, because we had to leave time to fill the hole and lug everything home before dark.

"Awww," I heard Charlie say to Roy, as they started gathering all the tools for the trek back.

I knew how he felt.

Packrat scooped up some dirt, and dropped it on the metal screen of the sifter.

Clink.

Crouched beside the most fun tool we had, I'd heard that *clink* as clearly as a barred owl hoot in the quiet of the night. I didn't know exactly what it was, but it was metal, which made it our last privy hole find.

I glanced up at Packrat. He grinned and nodded.

"Hey, Charlie?" I called, standing up and brushing the dirt off my knees. In a flash, he was at the edge of the privy hole, looking down at me.

"Yeah?"

"My arms are tired. Want to sift the last of it?"

He scrambled down faster than a cub from a tree.

Roy leaned on a shovel, watching from above. Packrat and I looked over Charlie's shoulder. He shook and shook and shook that sifter. I winked up at Roy, and he raised an eyebrow.

When the edge of the coin came into view, Charlie gasped. He shook the sifter one, two, three more times. Lifting it from the screen, he turned it over and over. He hesitated. Then he held it out to me.

It was well worn, and not shiny at all. But it had the year "1795" at the bottom. There was a lady's face, side view, in the middle, and the word LIBERTY over her head. There were five stars along the left side of the word, and five stars on the right of it.

"Whoa!" Packrat breathed.

It was pretty old. And it looked gold. It might be worth something. A lot of something.

I handed it back to Charlie. "Finders keepers," I told him.

Cooper and Packrat: Mystery of the Bear Cub

A week later, Roy and Packrat and I got to tag along with Warden Kate when she brought the bear family to our field. They'd had to tranquilize the mother bear to move her, and she was just now waking up in a big crate in the back of the warden's truck. Red was on the ground beside the truck in a smaller crate. Game Warden Kate had confirmed it; Red was a "he." And there he sat, looking a little fatter and more active than he had when we'd captured him and saved him from Talbot and Stu.

Warden Kate and a biologist had backed the truck up to the stone wall at the far end of the field. Just yesterday, the cleanup crew had finished hauling away the trash with bucket loaders and dump trucks. Then they'd leveled out the field almost to the way it had been. Now we could see chipmunks, ravens, and squirrels foraging like they should, free from the mounds of trash. All that remained was for the plant life to grow back again.

"No more seagulls in dental floss," Packrat said.

The three of us were sitting on top of the truck's cab, facing the back of the truck. Warden Kate wanted us up high when the mother bear came out.

"It was kinda fun helping all those animals, though." Roy looked a little like I felt—sort of sad to see another adventure wrapped up.

I looked off into the woods, toward the blueberry bushes. The berries would be ripe in two or three weeks, and I hoped the bears would stick around at least that long.

The mother bear made a low noise. The cub must have heard or sensed her, because he was making mewing noises and trying to look out of the slats of his own carrier.

Warden Kate opened the door of Red's crate. The cub backed up as far as he could. Warden Kate didn't pay him any mind. She turned to lower the tailgate of her truck before climbing into the bed behind the mother bear's crate. Reaching around, she opened the door and then stood back near us.

I held my breath.

Nothing happened.

"She needs a minute," Warden Kate whispered. "Once she gets moving, she'll take her cub to the woods and you'll have a new neighbor."

"Hey," I said, turning to Packrat and Roy, "that reminds me. Guess who's staying in town over the winter?"

Packrat grinned. "Charlie?"

"Yep! Mr. Goodwin offered Lynn a job at his store. He had heard me talking to Dad, and said it was time for him to take on a little help. She used to bake for her farm store, and he thought if she did that for him, and added some cinnamon rolls or something, it might bring in more business."

Roy licked his lips. "Cinnamon rolls!"

Red stuck his head out of the crate and cooed. The mother bear stuck her head out, too. Grunting twice, she shook her head. The cub stepped out and answered.

The mother bear ambled to the edge of the tailgate, swayed back and forth like she was judging the distance, then jumped down. The two of them met, the cub dancing around her, pawing her legs. She grunted again, and the cub followed her down the stone wall a ways. Suddenly, the cub stopped and sat. He scratched behind an ear, then got back up on his feet. The mother bear nuzzled her cub, pushing him with her nose, then nuzzling some more in a c'mon-let's-get-out-of-here kind of way.

A flash of black at the other end of the field caught my eye. The big bear! I jumped down into the bed of the truck to tug on the warden's sleeve. She turned to look.

We knew right away when that big male bear spotted the mother and cub. His ears perked up, and he moved toward them slowly. Like a predator, though, not like a neighbor welcoming a new family into the house next door. He stopped and sniffed the air, and took a few slow steps forward.

The mother bear put herself between this strange male and the cub. She made a low, pulsing growl, and the cub ran over to the nearest tree and climbed up about four feet before stopping to look back at his mom.

The male bear held his ground. The female took a few plodding steps toward the bigger bear. She stood on her hind legs, shook her head, and growled again. The male bear took a step back. And then another. Then he practically ran for the woods.

Warden Kate smiled. "I think this family is going to be all right."

"He moved out," Roy said quietly, his eyes still on the bears. "Dad. Months ago. I thought it was temporary—that he and Mom just needed a break, you know. Then, when he didn't come back, I thought I'd done something wrong."

Packrat and I started to talk at the same time, but Roy put up a hand to stop us.

"I know now that I didn't. But"—Packrat and I went still, as he continued—"he's not coming back."

Roy looked up at us. His voice got stronger as he talked.

"But we talked. Just like you said I should, Cooper. He promised to cut back on his hours. Work from his new apartment when I'm there. When the summer's over, I'll stay a week at his place and a week at Mom's."

I nodded. Not exactly what Roy had hoped for. Like he could read my mind, he shrugged and added, "Hey, I still have them both, just not in the same place at the same time. You were right. It could be worse."

The mother bear had gone to stand under the tree. She grunted, which I now knew was her call to come. At the dumpster, when she'd made that sound and paced around, she'd thought Red was still in there. Little did she know, he was here with us.

Red slid down the tree, butt first, landing in a heap at her feet. She nudged him with her nose, then led the way into the woods.

"On to the next adventure?" Packrat asked.

"Hope it's a good one!" Roy rubbed his hands together gleefully.

As long as I had my two friends with me, I knew any adventure would be a cool one.

"Last one to the canoe has to paddle all the way home!" I yelled, jumping off the back of the truck and racing for the trail.

I knew my friends would be right behind me.

They always were.

Author's Note

Dear Readers,

Have you ever traveled along a road and seen a plastic grocery bag hanging from a tree branch, caught there by the wind after being tossed away? Have you ever wondered how long it might stay there, if no one comes along to recycle it? Here's a list of some common items that people throw away, and how long they take to decompose:

Paper: 2 to 4 weeks

Cigarette butts: 1 to 5 years

Orange or banana peel: Up to 2 years

Wool socks: 1 to 5 years

Leather: 1 to 5 years

Plastic coated paper: 5 years

Plastic bag: 10 to 20 years

Nylon fabric: 30 to 40 years

Tin cans: 50 years

Aluminum can: 80 to 100 years

Plastic six-pack holder: 100 years

Monofilament fishing line: 600 years

Glass bottles: 1,000,000 years

Sources: Leave No Trace, USDA Forest Service, National Park Service

Acknowledgments

Whenever I hike or kayak, I can't help but look for signs of bear. Black bears. Honestly, though, if I were to run into one, I'm not sure what I'd do. My husband sternly says, "Leave the area immediately," which would be the wise thing, of course. But as you know by now, I'm such a nature geek, I'd probably raise my camera without even thinking twice.

Alas, in the twenty-six years that I've owned Poland Spring Campground, I've never seen signs of bear on the property. And the only bear report I've ever gotten from my campers was eighteen years ago, when they told of seeing a small bear swim across Lower Range Pond. It crawled out of the water onto my neighbor's property, then walked the shoreline toward town. Even if we had bears, the chances of studying them firsthand—as I've been able to do with eagles, foxes, and loons—would be slim. Black bears are experts at staying hidden from humans.

This, dear reader, was going to be a problem. As you know, I love to study my wildlife characters firsthand. I'm a visual learner, so I want to see for myself how they move. What sounds do they make? How do they act around each other? Around danger?

Could I see this on the computer—on YouTube, maybe? Sure. I could read about it in a book. I could ask an expert. And I did all those things. But there's nothing like seeing nature in action, in person, to get inspired.

One day, Lily Powell, a student writer in our After School Writing Club, gave me an idea. If I could not see the bears here at the campground, then I'd go to them. Lily's dad, Howie, manages the Maine Wildlife Park in Gray. Since all the animals at the park have been injured or have gotten used to humans, they can't be released back into the wild.

Lily reminded me about a special photographer pass the park issues. I went as a photographer not once, but twice. And I bought a yearly visitor pass, too. Not only would I get the research I needed, but the fees for the pass would also help these beautiful animals.

Guides Jade Kinard and Emilie Cram let me ask a thousand questions about the orphaned fox kits they'd just received. And the mountain lion kits. And the adorable little beaver. But it was the black bears at the Wildlife Park I most wanted to study. With my guide, I could stand on the bear's level to feel how tall they were. I was able to ask about the different colorings that black bears can have. I witnessed their rolling, plodding walk. I even got to feed one through the fence! Its tongue was long and sticky, its paws, huge!

After I soaked up all the inspiration I could, it was time to write. So very many people stood by my side in person or in spirit as I wrote *Mystery of the Bear Cub.* Whether it was a gift of encouragement when I needed it most, bear knowledge, or talking me through the rough patches, I am most grateful for their time and energy. And I'd like to take a moment to thank some of them here. As always, if I forget anyone, please forgive me. I do appreciate you all.

Of course, the minute they learned I was writing about bears, my Poland Spring Campground campers had a hundred and two stories to tell. Backyard bird feeders bitten in two. Cubs climbing into dumpsters. Bears startled on the trail. Poland Spring campers have the best campfire stories; I enjoyed each and every one!

Students and staff in all of RSU 16 are some of the most amazing people I know. And I'm not just saying that because they're some of the biggest Cooper and Packrat fans I know, too. From attending and throwing book launches, to reading and posting reviews, and designing Cooper and Packrat T-shirts, this author feels incredibly fortunate to have such a community in her corner.

And I can't pass up an opportunity to thank the students in Mrs. Shanning's room. You always asked how the writing was going, and cheered me on when the going was tough. And do you remember how surprised I was, when one of you brought in a bear skull to share during the first weeks of school? That was beyond cool.

Shannon, as always, you have been my friend through all the ups and downs and highs and lows on this project. Thank you for the many hours of manuscript reading and brainstorming. And thank you for always gently nudging me out of my comfort zone. You really would make a great publicist, you know.

In the final revision stages, I had this brilliant idea to have bear expert Deborah Perkins read the entire manuscript. In two weeks. And give me feedback. Not only did she accept, but she went above and beyond to help me make sure the bear behavior was realistic. And a special shout-out to Randy Cross, who answered e-mail questions, even during his busy, bear-banding season. I hope to thank you in person someday.

As I write this, the snow has melted, the loon pair has returned, and my thoughts turn to my Camp 'n Schmooze attendees. It's almost time for our spring retreat! You're all such very gifted writers, and I brag about you often. Cindy Lord, Carrie Jones, Val Giogas, Mona Pease, Jo Knowles, Denise Ortakales, Cindy Faughnan, Mary Morton Cowan, Laura Hamor, Jeanne Bracken, Nancy Cooper, Anna Jordan, Joyce Johnson, and Megan Frazer Blakemore . . . what would I do without all of you? I know you have my back, and I hope you know I have yours in return.

It takes many creative minds to take a story from idea to bookshelf, and I feel fortunate to have the entire staff at Islandport Press behind mine. From locating experts on the subject, planning author events, designing banners, to selling books—you are all so amazing at what you do. Thank you for loving Cooper and Packrat as much as I do.

Melissa Kim, you are one of the most patient people I know! This one was fun to edit, but that first draft—whew! Thank you for all your plotting help, and cheerleading. It wouldn't be the book it is today without your guidance.

Melissa Hayes, copy editor extraordinaire—as with Cooper's other adventures, I always feel better knowing you've had one last look to make sure everything is as it should be.

Carl DiRocco, you've done it again! The illustrations are perfect, as always. You're so very generous with your time and talent. No matter what crazy scheme I suggest, you're on board. I'm especially glad when we manage to find time to sign books together, as I love seeing our readers meet the guy who brings Cooper and Packrat to life.

Family is at the heart of every Cooper adventure, and I have one of the best. To the Wight and Lavallee clans, and the Piehls and the Watsons, the support and enthusiasm you've shown from Book 1 to Book 4 has never wavered or quieted. I hear you and adore you, even though there are many miles between us. XO.

Benjamin, thanks again for coming to my rescue when I needed a guy's perspective, especially with Roy and the Eight Ball pool table game in the game room scene. You are a constant source of inspiration to me, and I know you're going to fly off one day, to do great things. Never forget your return flight path, though. We'll be here.

Alexandra, I love nothing more than brainstorming ways to get Cooper in and out of trouble with you. You have amazing ideas, and I have no doubt that you'll write a grand novel someday, one that makes everyone sit up and take notice. And when you do, I hope I can help you in return.

And David, my hiking and kayaking companion: Who else could I call upon to go tromping on trails in warm weather, rain, and even March snow, to research abandoned cellar holes? I hope we have many, many more adventures together, all of them bigger than the last.

About the Author

Tamra Wight lives in Poland, Maine, where she has run the Poland Spring Campground with her husband and two children for twenty-five years. Every summer, at the campground, she meets interesting families from all over the world. During the school year, she works as a teaching assistant at Whittier Middle School. Between the two, she has more writing inspiration than she knows what to do with! She is the author of *Mystery on Pine Lake, Mystery of the Eagle's Nest,* and *Mystery of the Missing Fox,* the first three Cooper and Packrat adventures, as well as *The Three Grumpies* (illustrated by Ross Collins). When Tamra isn't writing, she enjoys wildlife watching, hiking, geocaching, kayaking, power-walking, and snowshoeing; most of these she does with her faithful lab Cookie. You can see her wildlife photos on her website, www.tamrawight.com.

Other Books from Islandport Press

The Door to January
By Gillian French

The Sugar Mountain Snow Ball
By Elizabeth Atkinson

The Five Stones Trilogy
By G. A. Morgan

Azalea, Unschooled
By Liza Kleinman

Lies in the Dust
By Jakob Crane and Timothy Decker